Lightning Struck

THE ROAMING CURSE
BOOK ONE

MIRANDA HARDY

Quixotic Publishing LLC
Royal Palm Beach, FL 33411
www.quixoticpublishing.com

Edited by: Keith B. Darrell
Cover by: Rebecca Frank

Lightning Struck/ Miranda Hardy. — First Edition

ISBN 978-1-939588-16-6 (print edition)
ISBN 978-1-939588-17-3 (eBook)

FOR
FAITH AND CODY

CHAPTER 1

THE LAST TIME I cried, thirteen people died. This is no place to sit and meditate, so I clear my mind and concentrate on controlling my emotions as the bus screeches to a stop next to me.

Elysia, focus on your surroundings. Dad's advice plays over in my head.

The wind whistles through the dark treetops in the park across the street and races toward me, sweeping my hair into a swirly mess. I tug on my hoodie as a shiver runs down my spine.

I breathe deeply, the early morning sounds heard before sunrise captivating my attention. As I listen intently, a frog croaks, splashing into the murky waters of a retention pond. Crickets chirp their familiar tune, reminding me of the swampy area we've called home for the past year.

I peruse the small, quiet station. The lone clerk behind the counter sips his coffee, yawns, and continues to look at his phone. The aroma of fried food mixed with the stench of garbage invades my senses. Next door, a cook from the diner brushes dirt from his hands before reentering through the side door.

Grabbing my duffel bag, I follow the young couple holding hands who are in line to board the bus. I silently pray I make it out of town. I'm used to being on the run, but this is the first time I'm running alone.

"Is this your first time going to New Orleans?" The young brunette chomps down on her gum, causing it to pop in her mouth.

"Huh?" It takes me a second to realize she's speaking to me.

"New Orleans? First time?" Her sweet southern accent and charming dimples stir a tinge of jealousy within me. She nibbles on her bottom lip.

"Oh, no." I mutter as we proceed to board.

"Isn't it the best? I mean, Baton Rouge is a bore compared to New Orleans." She continues talking as I show the driver my ticket. "We're just headin' up for the weekend. You know, getting out of town and seeing something different." Her eyes light up with enthusiasm.

I nod.

The two lovers sit in the front, making the back of the bus increasingly more appealing. I breath in the musty, heavy air and notice how old the bus is. The dark crimson seats need reupholstering, and cracks

2

creep up the dirty white restroom door.

As the driver releases the brakes, I plop down into the last seat in the rear.

New Orleans is only two hours from Baton Rouge, and the morning bus is devoid of many passengers, making the ride more tolerable.

I grip my duffel bag, remembering how Dad frantically shoved it into my arms and told me to leave. When he pushed me out the door and refused to let me back inside, I understood how dangerous things had become. I wish he had come with me as he always did, but I knew this time was different. We had stayed in Baton Rouge too long. I had made friends and started to settle, but settling isn't in the cards for us.

The bus jostles me back and vibrations tingle my feet through the soles of my sneakers.

Why was Dad so cryptic?

"Go. After I take care of a few things, I'll find you," he had said. Remembering the way he said it, his anger seeping through every word, gave me chills. It was so out of character for him. The hairs on my arms rise.

Out of the corner of my eye I see a flash of red. I turn to look out the back window. A black SUV with a red flashing light on its roof barrels onto the sidewalk of the bus station and two people jump out running into the tiny substation.

My heartbeat quickens and my skin flushes with heat. It's too hot on this damn bus. I'm thrown back as the brakes squeal. We've reached a red light. Talk about bad timing.

My hands sweat and bile rises up my throat. I know those people are looking for me.

The shadowy figures reappear next to the SUV. The driver points toward the bus as they hop in and pull out into the street. Panic grips me. I realize even if I got off, they'd see me. We've already passed the park where the trees could have provided some cover. There are only residential, one-story houses on either side of the street.

The light turns green. The bus lurches forward. The SUV is still two blocks away with its red light flashing.

The SUV swerves around a car in the intersection. A horn blares.

I'm trapped like a rat with a cat hot on my tail.

Then the rain starts—poor cat doesn't stand a chance.

CHAPTER 2

MY FEAR TRIGGERS a new threat: hail. The hail pounds on top of the bus, like rocks hitting a tin roof. A thick fog blankets the area. Dark clouds block the rising sun making it appear as dark as midnight.

"Where did that come from?" the young girl asks.

The bus slows. The driver leans toward the windshield, concentrating on the chaotic weather. I'm thankful the sound of the hail blocks out the siren coming up behind us.

The SUV swerves into the left lane. Its horn drowns in hail that now rips through the murky morning sky and hammers the vehicle like small shards of glass shattering on a tile floor. The quicker my heart beats the faster the hail comes.

The SUV's dim headlights scarcely appear visible in the thickening fog bank that envelopes it. It pushes faster, as the occupants ignore the possibility of hitting oncoming cars. My fear escalates and my hands shake as the black vehicle comes closer to the bus. At that moment, as if the Heavens hear my pleas, a large hailstone bashes in the windshield causing the SUV to veer off the road and ram into an oak tree.

The bus jerks forward again. The driver doesn't notice the crash we leave behind.

I close my eyes and breathe deeply, imagining a calmer place...a place from my past...a carousel of horses going round and round with an organ playing a marching tempo. The long metal silver pipes vibrate in the middle of the carousel, hypnotizing me. The vibrant colors of the horses appear as if they would rub off onto my fingertips. The fishy smell from the Atlantic Ocean invading my overactive senses make me want to ride the plastic horses into the depth of the ocean.

The hail stops hammering the roof, and the fog subsides illuminating the greenery on both sides of the bus. The clouds disperse, revealing the rising sun with its bright orange and red hues.

"That was weird," the young girl up front says. She glances from side to side.

I block her and everyone else on the bus out and wonder if I'll ever ride a carousel again. Regardless, it'll never be as marvelous as when I was younger and fascinated with the pipes playing music in the middle. Our imagination becomes less creative the older we get. I no longer dream of being a mermaid or fairy princess...my dreams now center on finding simplicity and consistency, neither of which I've ever had in my short twenty-two years.

The echoing brakes jostle me from a light slumber. In a haze, I look out the window and realize we're in New Orleans. The happy couple rush off the bus, as the driver wipes sweat from under his cap.

It's been eleven years since I've been to New Orleans and the unfamiliar streets look intimidating. The cab stand sits thirty feet away and that's the quickest possible route out of the bus station. There's no telling how far behind the Hunters may be or if they are here already.

A slow rain trickles as I race toward the empty line. I realize my heart beats faster than usual at the thought of being caught here. A man stands against the first cab and looks up at the wet threat.

"Can you take me to the..." I stop myself from saying the name of the hotel. My father's warning blares in my head. *Leave no obvious path, Elysia.* "Umm, the House of Blues please."

"Cha, but I don't think it open, yet." The bronze skinned cab driver opens the door to the back seat.

"Oh, I'm meeting a friend." I toss my duffel bag on the seat and slide in. The rain falls faster.

He nods and rushes to the driver's seat. Although it'll cost more for a taxi than it did for the $11 bus ticket from Baton Rouge, this is the best decision. The House of Blues is several blocks and a street over from the meeting place; I'm proud I remembered to direct him there instead of where I actually need to go.

As we pass a few streetlights, the rain subsides. I'm filled with relief. The streets take on a more familiar look. I try to remember when I was here last. Although New Orleans isn't far from Baton Rouge, it seems worlds apart. Often, my coworkers would travel here to party for a weekend. They invited me a few times, but I always said no…too scarred from my previous memories of living here, I suppose.

When I was eleven, Dad and I lived in a small one-bedroom apartment just north of New Orleans. He helped manage the apartment building to get a discount on our rent. The residents used the onsite laundry room because the units didn't have a washer/dryer. The swingset was worn and often broken so I'd play hide-n-go-seek a lot with some of the other kids that lived there.

The kids thought I was lucky I didn't have to go to school with them, but I was always jealous seeing them get on the bus in the morning. That jealousy led to one of the worst events I've ever caused and it saddens me to think about it…1,836 deaths and billions of dollars in damage all because of my anger with my father over not allowing me to go to school with the other kids.

Hurricane Katrina should have been called Hurricane Elysia.

Years later, when I turned thirteen and my pubescent turbulence caused wildfires in California, my father sat me down and told me about my "gift". It seemed like a curse to me, and still does. That's when I started writing down all the statistics related to the disasters I caused wherever we lived. I've since memorized them...my journals always seemed to be left behind when we moved.

"You're here, Miss." The cab stopped in front of the House of Blues Restaurant & Music Hall. The unlined two-way street looks desolate in the early hour.

"Thank you." I hand him a twenty dollar bill, which offers him a nice tip.

"Ya sure ya meeting someone?" he asks.

I nod.

"Okay, then. Have a good day, Miss." He drives down the deserted street, leaving me to stare at the blue HELP lighted sign above a door. How appropriate.

The hot air feels thicker than normal. Flipping the duffel bag on my shoulder, I go east hoping I'm headed in the right direction. I pass Dollz & Dames, looking in the windows at the shoes lined up, wishing I were here on a shopping trip. HELP EVER HURT

NEVER…the rest of the saying above the door and windows of the House of Blues building. I have no idea what that means. I continue down the street, past the box office entrance.

The candy store on the corner looks enticing, but I keep walking hoping to find the street I need. A woman jogs by as the next intersection comes into view. It's the right street and my shoulders relax. Conti Street.

The dirty one-way street is in need of a good paint job. Red and blue dumpsters line the west side with a few empty cars parked on it. As I pass a parking area between two tall buildings, my duffel bag becomes heavier. When I reach Conti and Chartres, I worry and wonder if I'm headed in the right direction. It feels like I've walked for hours. The area looks nicer now with restaurants lining the street and wider sidewalks.

The street narrows. I try to imagine what it looks like in the evening with a swarm of people flooding the area. Watching the sidewalks, I'm sure I've stepped over more than a few puke stains in the last block…gross. Several hotels come into view; I become discouraged each time it's not the one I need. I underestimated the distance, thinking it would be an easier march than this. A drizzle of water falls down my cheek.

Don't panic. Don't panic.

LIGHTNING STRUCK

My pace quickens as I shift the duffel bag to my other shoulder. British, American, and French flags wave in the breeze on a second-story balcony. The hotel sign under three red awnings is a welcome sight. A man hoses down the sidewalks in front of some German restaurant across the street, and I want to jump for joy…I've made it to my destination.

A club-type restaurant and bistro lines the south side, opening into a courtyard. My stomach growls; the Creole food smells enticing.

The hotel entrance is on the north side of the walkway between the two buildings. The open right door leads into a fancy sitting area with a marble coffee table and high diamondback chairs in front of a black leather couch. A lit, curved chandelier overhead reminds me of an elaborate display of Christmas fairy lights.

A plump, smiling Creole woman stands behind the creamy counter, and a large display of postcards and brochures sit under the windows nearby.

"What can I do ya for?" She yawns and scratches her nose.

I place my duffel bag under the counter. "I'd like to check in, please." I reach into my purse and pull out my wallet. "Lili Williams." Dad always said I looked like a Lili. It's an emergency name we haven't had to use in any city we've lived in.

"Check-in isn't till four, but let me see what we

have." The stout lady sighs and clicks the computer keys. "One night?"

I tilt my head down, trying to decide if that's enough. I honestly don't have much money for too many nights. The tips from last night are shoved deep in my jean pocket.

"We have the Deluxe Two Queens room available for you." She looks up to me through her fake eyelashes.

"That's fine."

"You're lucky I'm here now...it was a crazy party night and we usually end at 5:30. It's been slow lately, though." She clicks away on her keyboard. "It's $129 per night plus tax."

I hand her my ID and cash. She swipes the keycard for me and provides a paper holder for it with the room number written on it.

"Check-out's 11AM. Have a good day now, ya hear."

She forces a smile. I pick up my duffel bag and head to the dark glass elevator. The doors open to a mirrored box outlined with gold trim and rails. An advertisement for the club hangs on the left of the doors.

Sconces line the third-floor hallway and the raggedy, flowered carpet looks as if it hasn't been replaced in decades. The doors are freshly painted in the cream-themed color with florid designs over them. My room is next to the exit sign.

The squashed room holds two beds, an armoire, and a desk. It doesn't have a balcony, of course, but the view of the courtyard is cozy to look at. I throw my purse and the duffel bag on the bed. My nervousness kept me from opening the duffel bag on the bus, but it's time to see what Dad packed.

I pull out several tops and jeans. An envelope falls onto the covers. I can barely control my shaking hands to open it. My chest constricts; raindrops hit the window. I take a deep breath as I slide out the folded piece of paper.

> *Dear Elysia,*
>
> *Seeing you blossom in Baton Rouge this past year made my heart happy. You made friends and smiled more than I've ever seen. It pains me to think you've not been afforded the same opportunities that others get. You've not been able to go to college under your real name, yet I'm so proud of you for taking the courses you enjoy most just to learn. You would've been a skilled ecologist if given the chance.*
>
> *I blame myself for the things you've not been able to do, and you've never blamed me for it or questioned me or my guidance. When the feeling to flee surfaced a few days ago, I ignored it. I was praying it was false and would pass, as we've been here longer than any other place. I*

13

cried. I cried for you, mostly. Another place to settle, more friends to leave, a new job to find – this isn't the life I'd want for my worst enemy, let alone for you – the only one I love on this planet.

I'm tired Elysia. I'm tired of running and moving. I'm sorry I ignored the call so long this time. I may have compromised us...I may have compromised you and I apologize for that, but I need to end this. We can't keep running forever. I'm hoping to stop them from chasing us. If I succeed, I'll see you soon. If I fail...I won't fail.

Love you,

Dad

The rain pelts the windows, as tears fall down my face. The rain continues...for three days. My sadness shows in the constant patter of the water on the stones below and the ominous clouds in the sky; and then an unexpected anxiousness boils in my stomach as I hear the knocks at the door.

CHAPTER 3

K NOTS FORM IN my stomach as I near the door, wondering if the person knocking wants to kill me or hug me. The conversation Dad and I had when I was thirteen replays in my head.

"The Hunters want to destroy what we are," Dad explained.

"What are we?" I asked

"We're Roma and our abilities scare people. It's a cruel world, Elysia. People fear what they do not understand."

He kissed me on the cheek and hushed any further questions I wanted to ask. Dad was a man of few words and didn't waste time with what he referred to as "nonsense talk".

The impatient knocker pounds harder. "Delivery!" a loud female voice booms. My heart skips a beat...I didn't order anything.

Creeping toward the door, I peer through the peephole and see the lady from the front desk. I can't see if she's holding anything, but surely, after being here three days, she's not one of the Hunters, otherwise I'd be dead by now.

As I reach for the doorknob, an envelope slides under the door tapping my foot. Heavy footfalls echo down the hallway. I let out a breath I didn't realize I was holding. The envelope has only my room number on it. I pick up the bulky, heavy cream envelope and wonder how it even fit under the door.

The phone rings and I literally jump back against the wall. To say I'm on edge is an understatement. Crazy thoughts roam my head…what if the Hunters caught Dad and they are using him to find me? What if Dad is trying to warn me to leave and I'm ignoring his call? What if the Hunters are checking to see if I'm in the room so they can barge in and grab me or maybe waiting for me to leave?

"Stop this!" I sit on the unmade bed, rip the letter open, and let the phone go to the message center or front desk…whatever they have here. A few hundred dollar bills and several twenties fall onto the floor. Inside the envelope is a notecard with a name and address on it, along with a scribbled message.

Simza Kepi ~ Cassadaga, Florida…
Make sure no one learns of your ability…no one!

Kepi happens to be my middle name. That's

strange. It was my mother's last name too...I'm sure of it. Is this a relative I didn't know about? Is Dad directing me to go find this person?

The phone rings again.

"Hello?"

"Get out of there now. They're coming for you." A deep female voice says. Then a click...she's gone.

"Oh, hell no!" I slam the phone down, grab the few things I have and throw them into the duffel bag in under a minute flat, and leave the hotel room...the place I was hoping to meet Dad. I've already stayed two days longer than I should have. Fear takes over ever cell in my body when I realize I may never see him again.

Bolting out the door, I hear the elevator ding down the hall. A woman steps out wearing a black leather pantsuit. Her jet black hair hangs straight to her shoulders and her arched eyebrows hide under short bangs. Her gaze finds me when she looks down the hall in my direction. We both pause staring at each other. She scrunches her face.

A twinge in my gut tells me she's looking for me and she's a Hunter...I feel it and it annoys me I don't know how I know...I just do. Her eyes narrow and recognition seeps into her face, causing her hardened countenance to ease.

She points to me. "The Girl!"

Anger boils to the surface of my skin.

My senses sharpen as she reaches for something behind her. That's my cue to race across the hall, through the stairway door and down as fast as I can. Heavy footfalls sprint down the carpet and the second-story door thunders open as I reach the door on the first floor.

"Shit!" Her curse echoes in the stairwell right before I open the first-floor door. I didn't see her companion, but I'm sure there are only two of them.

I bust through the door with no regard for what or who may be on the other side and race through the courtyard toward the crowded street. The duffel bag quickly becomes heavy on my tense shoulder. A car horn blares at me as I dash in front of them. People's heads turn my way as I reach the other side of the street. I slow my pace and peer over my shoulder to see the dark-haired woman leaving the hotel courtyard. She spots me and I pick up my pace.

Turning the first corner I come to, I see the woman's male companion moving in the opposite direction. Both of them are on my trail, fast and ready to take me down. They want to block me between them, so I run again across a busy street, between two cars and move back onto Conti Street.

The lunchtime crowds push me into the swell of the street. I maneuver around them. Looking back, I see the woman talking into her phone as she gains on me. I pick up my pace. The further down the street I get, the less crowded it becomes. I cross over Conti again to get closer to the construction side of things. Maybe I can cut through the buildings and get further away from her.

My heartrate quickens and shadows appear under my feet as dark clouds begin to move in.

Pockets of the lunch goers block the woman on the other side of the street. I round a dumpster and find a break between two buildings to enter. It's an empty parking lot, blocked off for construction of the building that's lining the next street over. The workers are not on site, luckily. I cross over a dirt pile and get behind a large cement post.

The open building seems to be the beginning of a parking structure and doesn't provide much cover between the buildings on either side. I take too long to decide if I should continue forward and try to make it to one of the buildings for better cover. I hear someone traipsing through the dirt around the dumpster.

"I'm sure she went through the buildings. Hurry around, damn it! We can't lose her again." The snarky, out-of-breath voice sounds irritated. I can tell she's not a track star if she's losing her breath on this short jaunt. This gives me an edge. I'm sure I can outrun her if need be, but she's too close right now, and by the way she reached behind her short coat earlier in the hall, there's a good chance she has a gun.

A few more steps and she'll see my hiding place.

My mind races with possible escape tactics. If I move slowly around the exterior of the beam, maybe she will bypass me without notice. She's too close now.

Blood rushes to my cheeks and rage builds within me.

She passes the beam. I drop my duffel bag. She whirls around and reaches for the clip attached to the back of her dark jeans that holds her gun. The top of my foot slams into her hand. Shock replaces recognition on her face. It's much different kicking a person rather than breaking a stiff board, but I didn't hesitate. All of the martial arts training and kickboxing Dad insisted on was worth it. She falls face first into the gray dirt; the gravel scrapes her cheeks and blood trickles down the right side of her face.

"Mother—" she cuts off the curse word that is about to erupt from her pissed-off mouth as I yank the gun out of the belt before she has a chance to turn over.

Thunder breaks through the stormy clouds, mirroring my rage as it seeps through my skin.

She holds her hands up, palms open. "Now, we only wanted to have a little chat with you." She doesn't hide the fury in her squinty, copper eyes.

LIGHTNING STRUCK

"Your chat requires holding me at gunpoint?" I narrow my eyes to match hers, and hold up the gun in my left hand, allowing it to dangle on my finger by the trigger. I've never fired a gun and I don't like the feel of it in my hand now. I want to throw it as far away as possible, but I can't allow her to see my nervousness.

"Merely a precaution." She squats and stands.

Cars pass on the other side of the unfinished cement structure. I remember her partner is nearby. I can take her out, but I'm not sure how I'd fair against the duo.

"A precaution you take with everyone you want to meet or simply those you fear?" I smirk.

Her mouth twists and her jaw tightens. Her face turns crimson. It's obvious I hit a nerve.

"If you think I fear you, you'd be sadly mistaken." She grins and folds her arms.

The thunder roars above. "Where's my father?"

Breaking our eye contact, she looks at the fuming clouds that matches my seething brain.

"I don't know." She glances toward the street. "But, maybe if you come with us, you'll see him again soon."

The Hunters want us dead. Dad's words echo in my head.

"Somehow I don't think that's the wisest choice for me." My lips press. I drop the gun. Her gaze follows it to the ground as my right hook swings into her cheek knocking her out on the dirt floor.

The sting from the punch pulses in my fist, but the adrenaline coursing through my veins pushes me to move. I grab my duffel bag and double back to Conti Street and into the crowd as the rain begins to fall.

It's time to pay this Simza Kepi a visit to find out who called to warn me about the Hunters. Someone other than Dad is keeping me alive and there's a good chance they can help me find him.

CHAPTER 4

IT'S STRANGE I'M headed into the one place Dad said we should never live again…the peninsula of Florida.

In 2004 we lived in Panama City Beach. Dad worked as a handyman for vacation rental properties. He'd often take me to work with him and I'd play at the white, sandy beach on the Gulf.

Being 10, all I wanted to do was create sandcastles and pretend I was a mermaid. It felt natural being outdoors and near the ocean. Each morning, I'd make Dad's coffee and toast to hurry him out of our tiny apartment so I could get to the beach.

The summer had ended and only one family was vacationing at the beach. The only reason I remember is they had a daughter my age. Dad insisted I play with her because she didn't have any siblings to play with.

She tormented me for three days. The last straw was when she pushed me down into my newly-made sandcastle. Hurricane Ivan headed straight for us; I couldn't control my anger and it smacked straight into the coast.

Dad said living anywhere in Florida would be a disaster. I hope he was wrong.

* * *

It would be nice to take a plane some time instead of traveling by bus. Planes fascinate me…getting to a specific destination in hours instead of days would be great. Dad thought it was too dangerous for me to be high in the air with the chance my emotions might run amok. I quickly imagine a sudden flash of lightning striking a plane and shake my head to clear the image away.

There are no bus depots in Cassadaga, so the closest station is in Sanford, which takes me 18 miles south of where I need to be. Instead of traveling straight to Cassadaga, I find the closest library.

Cassadaga: *"The Psychic Capital of The World"*.

"This should be interesting," I whisper while staring at the computer screen. Searches on the area reveal a small "spiritual camp" with a limited history on the town. Of course, there is no listing for Simza

Kepi.

"Why is nothing easy?"

She's also not found in any searches in nearby towns or on any phone records.

The intercom switches on. "The library will close in five minutes."

"Wonderful." The old woman at the information desk lifts her chin and watches me.

According to the Calendar of Events on the spiritual camp page, I may be able to make the Orb Spirit Encounter that starts at 7:30PM. I print the directions to the camp, grab my duffel bag, and head for the exit, passing the looming old woman's judgmental stare on my way out.

I'm going to have to do some old-fashioned detective work to find Simza.

***

The Uber driver drops me off in front of the bookstore at exactly 7:25PM and the desolate parking lot indicates it's not a hot tourism spot for the area. One would think the Psychic Capital of the World would be able to predict the best times to hold tours and events.

I chuckle and shake my head.

The building across the street has a few vehicles parked on the side. It's set up like a small, middle

American town, but with a touristy feel. Signs litter both buildings displaying various medium names. There's also a sign for BINGO. That sounds fun…if you're 40 years older than me.

A four-door white sedan parks in one of the empty parallel parking spots. Two older ladies get out and chat while they make their way into the bookstore. I follow closely.

"I don't know why I'm doing this," the golden-gray-haired woman says to her friend.

"Because you have nothing better to do." The white-haired woman with the camera hanging around her neck snorts and laughs. Her friend grins.

"Hello." An older lady with dyed blonde hair smiles as we enter the bookstore. "Are you ladies here for the Orb Encounter?"

"We sure are," the camera-wielding woman in front of me replies.

I nod.

She takes our "contributions", our names, and offers to hold my duffel bag in the back room, which I wholeheartedly accept after taking my purse out of it.

The warm night, mixed with the humidity is nothing new to me, but the sounds are different…crickets and insects swarm near us while we remain outdoors. Several people smack at the mosquitos that don't bother with my Rom blood.

LIGHTNING STRUCK

There are more people than I thought interested in this outing. Some walked from the nearby hotel, which explains the lack of cars in the front.

The tour is uneventful. The guide talks about the history of Cassadaga and shows us several spots that spirits tend to roam. Everyone takes pictures except me. I had grabbed a newsletter from the counter that contained all the mediums/psychics in the camp, hoping Simza Kepi would be one of them, but she isn't listed.

It's almost 10:00PM and several visitors head back to their hotel.

"Excuse me." I wait for the two older ladies to move away from the tour guide. "I'm looking for a Simza Kepi. I was told she lives around here. Do you know her?"

Her loose, steel-gray hair brushes her cheek as she processes my question. She shakes her head. "I've not heard of her. I'm sorry."

"Thank you." I grab my duffel bag and leave the bookstore, wondering where I'll go from here.

"Hi." The golden-gray-haired woman smiles at me. "I overheard you asking for Simza. I've heard that name before, but I don't think she lives in Cassadaga."

"You have?" My face relaxes and I feel a shred of hope.

She nods. "I'm quite sure I've heard that name."

She leans in and whispers. "I think she talked to my dead husband."

"Huh?" The hope I felt didn't last too long.

"What are you telling that girl, Mavice?" her white-haired companion asks.

"Shhh…why do you have to be so cotton-pickin' loud, Maxine?" Mavice waves her hand up and down toward her companion. She grabs my free hand and pats it. "She's the real deal, but she goes by a different name. She's not associated with this place. She came into town a few months ago. I'm certain she was talking to my Harold."

"She's a psychic?" I ask.

She shakes her head. "Not really. She talks to the dearly departed. I guess she's a true medium. I've had many readings here, but not like with Madam Aishe."

"Madam Aishe?" I ask.

Her expression hardens. "That's her stage name, I reckon, because I recall her sister called her Simza while I was waiting for a reading. Maybe that's the woman you're looking for?" She asks. "Simza isn't a real popular name." She gave a half-smile.

"Where does she live?" I ask.

"You're not from around here, are you dear?" She looks at my duffel bag.

"Just got into town." I shrug.

"Well, we'll take you there. It's so late now." Mavice looks up into the sky, the half-moon peeking through the shadowy clouds.

"That would be amazing." I smile.

"What are we doing?" a puzzled Maxine asks.

"Oh, it's on our way home, Maxine." Mavice opens the back door for me.

The ladies were curious, asking my age, where I came from, and why I was looking for Simza. I'm sure they were trying to make me feel more welcome, but my lies kept flowing as they usually do.

I'm glad they gave me a ride, because there was no way I could have found this place.

Hanging moss covers the trailer and RV park sign. The ladies drop me off at the entrance and Mavice tells me it's the trailer at the far end of the park with the hanging red lanterns surrounding the awning.

The crickets play their music as I walk in the darkness. One light shines down over the park office, but the lights inside aren't on. The closed sign hangs behind the window.

Some illumination gleams through a few of the RVs and their generators buzz. One fire dies down at one of the spots, but most are empty. A few trailers seem more permanent than the others, with fresh gardening aligning their walkways. I wonder if the one in front is the grounds manager who lives here year-round since her garden sign says "Home Sweet Home".

Nearing the dirt path that marks the last street in the park, I notice a few empty cabins. Pine trees provide a canopy over the outer edges of the park that gives it an eerie feeling without street lamps to light the darkness.

The trailer with the red lanterns glowing at the end of the street reminds me of a metal tin can. It's one that needs to be pulled with a vehicle. The rusty, maroon truck parked next to it is probably the companion that makes it mobile.

I drop my duffel bag on the concrete slab that houses the metal cylinder on wheels. I breathe in and out, my nerves on edge as I climb the rickety stairs to the oval door. Before I chicken out, I knock on the door and get off the stairs quickly.

Footsteps shake the trailer and the door swings out.

"Yes?" The tall, willowy woman with an elongated face squints. She wears a long flowery orange skirt that reaches her ankles and a pair of brown sandals wrap her feet. Her shirt cuts off at the midriff and silver coin chains hang around her neck, covering her bosom.

"Are you Simza Kepi?" My voice shakes.

Her jaw drops and her expression dulls. She lets out a loud breath. "There's nothing for you here. Leave." She slams the door.

CHAPTER 5

BIG RAIN DROPS threaten to drown my sorrow. One hits my cheek, mixing with a tear.

"You okay, sweetie?" A soft voice carries in the wind. I turn to see a petite, stout woman smiling at me. Her smile fades. She purses her lips together. "You need a place to stay, don't you?"

I wipe my tear away and stare at this strange, curious woman. What a uncanny thing to ask, but the duffel bag probably gave away my predicament. "I'll be okay."

She looks up at the dark sky and blinks into the heavy, slow drops.

"Of that, I have no doubt." I think she winks at me since the side of her face scrunches up, but the darkness hides the gesture. "Follow me." She turns briskly walking from the camper.

"Okay." She leads me to one of the cabins off in

the tree lines.

"I just knew I'd be needing this place ready today. I spent the entire day cleaning it for you."

"Excuse me?" This place gets weirder by the moment.

She giggles, stops, and faces me. "I'm sorry. Sometimes I say the silliest things that make no sense to people. It's a bad habit." She reaches her hand out toward me. "I'm Deena. I manage this park."

I shake her hand. "Alice."

"Hmm, I didn't peg you for an Alice." She turns, walks up the stairs of the first cabin, and unlocks the door.

"How did—"

"How did I know you needed a place to stay?" she asks. "Oh, it's in the stars. I knew a stranger would come this way today seeking shelter." She looks up through the pine trees toward the sky. "It's a gift."

"I don't have a lot of money. I don't know what you charge." I follow her into the cabin as the rain falls faster, thankful for her gift.

"I think we'll figure something out. I have a feeling you'll be here for a little while." Deena hands me the key. "I put some things in the fridge. I figured you'd be hungry."

"Umm, thank you." My eyes narrow. My mind flutters with confusion. "How'd ya—"

"How'd I know you'd need food? Just a hunch. I get them from time-to-time." Deena's mouth twists into a half-smile.

"Do you know Simz…Madam Aishe?" I put my duffel bag on the floor and the key on the kitchen counter.

She glances to the ceiling. I follow her gaze. The wooden fan looks like long leaves going slowly in circles. "She's been here a few months, always pays her rent on time, but I try to stay away. The dead really freak me out."

"Everything is beginning to freak me out here."

"Well, you are in the psychic capital, you know." She grins and walks to the door. "I'll stop by tomorrow and check on you. We can work something out then."

I nod. She closes the door behind her. I stare at the clean cabin. The kitchen is small with a fridge, sink, a few cabinets, and a stove with a microwave above it. The tiny living room has a sofa, loveseat, coffee table, and a small TV on a wooden stand. I walk further down a hall and see a bedroom with a double bed and dresser. The bed looks freshly made with an extra pillow laid at the end of it.

I've officially entered the *Twilight Zone*.

***

The early sunrise, mixed with the pine scent through the open window and the birds chirping, makes me want to stay in bed a little longer and enjoy that simple moment of carefree bliss where all my problems don't exist.

A knock at the door makes the blissful moment evaporate into thin air.

"Rise and shine sleepyhead." Deena's squeaky voice permeates the cabin space. "I've got a treat for you."

"Coming." I drag myself out of bed and slip on my sandals. Before opening the door, a whiff of a decadent cinnamon reaches my nostrils. "Oh, that smells good."

Deena stands in front of the door with a platter of moist rolls. My stomach growls.

"Yes, I baked them fresh. No sense in buying store-bought when you have a recipe this good." She places the aluminum pan on the stove.

"Thank you." I take one of the cabin plates out of the cupboard and help myself.

In the daylight, it's easier to see Deena's sharp honey eyes and her ash brown spiral curly hair. She's probably a few inches shorter than my 5'5" stature. Her baby face makes her look younger than I think she may be.

"You're welcome, Alice." She smirks and it immediately makes me think she doesn't believe that's my name. That's never happened before.

"Have you always been psychic?"

"Oh, I'm not psychic." Her face brightens.

"Then how did you know I was coming?" I chomp down on the cinnamon roll and let the warm icing slither down my throat. This is the best I've ever had.

The corners of her eyes crinkle. "It's my intuition. You know we have a lot more senses than the five they teach us about in school."

"Is that so?"

She leans against the kitchen counter and places her hands on her chin. "Oh yeah. We've been taught to suppress what we don't know or understand, but if you train yourself, you can learn how to use your other senses."

She seems so sure of herself and honest.

"This is delicious, by the way." I take another bite.

She nods. "Oh, I know." She sits up and pats her round belly.

I chuckle.

"So, do you want the grand tour of the place?" she asks.

"Sure." Her mood lifts my spirits...so positive, happy, and sure of herself. Her energy is contagious.

I grab the key, follow Deena out of the cabin, and lock up. Dad was a stickler for locking the front door and it rubbed off.

"It's a small campground and it's off season now, so there's not a lot of people staying here." She walks down the path past the pine tree line. "Actually, it's off season all the time. We are a hidden gem here surrounded by woods. Not a lot of nature left in Florida, especially down south. Too many transplants from up north and such."

"How long have you been here?" I ask.

"Oh, I've been here two years now, I guess. Not long."

Simza's silver cylinder trailer glistens under the morning sun with moisture. Her truck sits next to it, so I assume she's home. She's not going to get rid of me that easily.

"I moved here to get away from the city life and get back in touch with nature." Deena points toward her trailer. "That really belongs to the owner, but he was nice enough to provide it as housing for the right manager, and that's me."

"Where's the owner?"

"He lives in upstate New York. I've only met him once." She kicks a pine cone off the dirt street that leads to the front of the campground. "One of those rich men who inherited his parents' fortune. He said he didn't know what to do with this place. Tried to sell it a few times, but no takers. Not profitable enough, he said."

LIGHTNING STRUCK

The campground is square with woods surrounding it. One dirt road leads toward the street I was dropped off last night. A small building meets the entrance with a fenced-in pool behind it. I hadn't seen the pool in the darkness last night.

"We have laundry facilities." Deena points toward the back of the building. "Only two washers and dryers, coin operated, of course." She shrugs. "The pool is well maintained and refreshing on the hot days."

"Looks nice."

"Yeah, it's a nice little place, isn't it?" I follow her to the front door. She unlocks it. "Here's the office, which I'm in most of the time, but I always see visitors when they come in since my trailer is not far away."

"You saw me come in last night?"

"Yeah, I heard the car drive up." She shuffles some papers. "You don't need a key or anything to get into the pool area; the fence is always unlocked."

The small office can't be more than the size of the cabin I stayed in last night. One cooler sits in a corner stocked with soda, water, and juice. A display of candy, marshmallows, graham crackers and chips hang on the wall next to it.

"This is nice." I see a price list written on a chalkboard behind the wooden counter.

Plain site/no-electric $20

Site with electric	$30
Cabin	$45

"It's cozy to me." Deena flips on the overhead fluorescent light. "I was thinking you can stay in the cabin for a weekly rate of $150 cash? Is that okay?"

"Really?" I point to the sign. "That's not even four nights."

"Well, I said cash, didn't I?" She grins. "I need to eat too, and the owner doesn't pay me."

"I see." I smile. "You're skimming off the top."

"Don't go telling anyone though. I don't do this often and not for just anyone. There's something special about you, Alice." She twirls her hair and squints her eyes. "I don't know what it is about you yet, but I can tell you need to be here."

"Well, you've convinced me." I dig in my pocket, and slap down $150 for the first week. "Can I ask you about how to find a job around here?"

She grabs a piece of paper with a map on it from under the counter and circles a spot "Here's the bus route. It stops in front of the grounds and takes you directly into town. It's a small town, but it has character. They might have a few places you can look there."

"What about Cassadaga?" I ask.

"Nah, you won't find much there, unless you're a tarot card hack or tea leaf reader. They are more 'spiritual' than psychic, really." She giggles. "Always good for entertainment purposes."

"They're not real psychics in the Psychic Capital?"

"They are as real as people need them to be." Deena follows me to the door and walks outside with me.

"Thank you for this." I hold up the map and turn to head back to Simza's trailer. Might as well demand a few answers before I head into town.

"It's my pleasure."

I swing my head around and see Deena looking at the clear blue sky, not a cloud covering an inch of it. An old silver Camaro pulls into the campground; its brakes squeak as it slows. Deena looks at the driver intently and then back to the sky. "Better bring an umbrella, Alice. There's a storm coming."

CHAPTER 6

THE WOMAN APPROACHES Simza's trailer, stops short when she spots me, takes out a tomato from her brown paper grocery bag and hurls it at me. It smacks me in the leg and tomato juice stains my jeans. "What the fuck?"

"You're not going to haunt me, Lyuba. Haunt Simza all you want, but not me." She takes out another tomato. "What did I do to you? Nothing!"

"Whoa, lady, stop that right now!" I point at her. Thunder erupts from the newly-formed gray clouds above. Her glare remains on me.

Her tense shoulders relax. She lowers the tomato. "You're not Lyuba, are you?"

"No, I'm not Lyuba." It dawns on me in that moment when I speak her name…she's talking about my mother.

The tomato hurler drops it to the ground and

inches closer to me. A tear rolls down her cheek. "You look so much like her."

The clouds break and a calmness overcomes me. "My mother?"

She wraps her arms around me, and mumbles something into my hair.

"Huh?" I pat her back, but I'm not fully committed. And, I wonder why she's mad enough at my mom to throw tomatoes at her.

"I'm your Aunt Mirela...Lyuba's sister." She pulls back, her hands squeeze the sides of my upper arms. "I thought you were dead."

"I'm—"

"I don't even know your name, chavi." She releases me.

I flounder. Confusion floods my mind. I don't know if I should tell her my real name or continue with this new persona. It's probably best to have her call me Alice since she's slipped with Simza's name. "It's Aaa...Alice."

"Well, Alice, it's nice to meet you." She backs away, still staring at me. "How did you find us?"

"It's a long story."

"Did you talk with Simza...your Aunt Simza?" She looks at the trailer and back at me.

"Not exactly. I tried last night, but she wasn't keen on speaking with me." A curtain flutters in the corner of my eye and I realize Aunt Simza witnessed

41

our exchange, but doesn't come outside.

Aunt Mirela wears a solid light baby blue long skirt, with a pretty low-cut black tank top. Her shiny, black sandals have rhinestones on the sides. Her caramel hair and olive skin remind me of my mother.

"She's become very antisocial in her old age." She picks up the bag and bangs on the door. "Open up Sim; I know you're in there."

"Go away, Mirela; and tell her to go away, too," Aunt Simza hollers through the door.

"That 'her' is your niece, you know." She bangs on the door again and waits a few moments. "Fine, but you'll have to show your face sooner or later. You can't stay fuming at everyone all of the time."

Hard footfalls stomp away informing us she's done with the conversation.

"She'll come around." Aunt Mirela's mouth twitches. "She's mad at me over a trivial matter. Always so stubborn, the old mule."

"I was given her name." I pull out the note from my pocket and show it to Aunt Mirela.

"So, that's what brought you to town. Who gave you this?"

"I honestly have no clue." A part of me wants to let loose and tell her everything, and ask a million other questions roaming through my head about this family I never knew I had.

"Curious." She hands the note back to me and

studies my face for a moment too long. "Come with me. I'll cook for you and you can meet your cousins."

"Cousins?" Flutters erupt from my stomach. My father never mentioned I had aunts or cousins. He told me we were alone.

"Well, are you coming?" Aunt Mirela stands next to the open driver side door.

"Yes." I rush to the car and wonder what's in store for me.

***

The drive to my newly-discovered Aunt's place took less than 10 minutes. A large oak tree towers over a manufactured home, nestled on at least an acre. No neighbors are in sight, so it appears they value their privacy. Aunt Mirela parks next to a white, older Mercedes in front of their place.

"Your place is nice."

"It does the job." She takes out more bags that lay on the backseat.

"Let me help." I grab one out of her hands.

"Thank you, Alice." The corner of her mouth turns up. "It's nice to see someone your age with manners."

A red truck skids into the yard blowing up dirt and stops on the other side of the Mercedes. A lanky, snub-nosed guy gets out. "Hey, Ma." He waves and his head turns in our direction. He stares at me. "Hey there to you." His chin rises and he winks.

"Don't flirt with your cousin, Emilian." She smacks him on the side of his head.

His jaw drops. "Cousin? What cousin? We have no cousins." He raises his arms in the air and follows us inside.

A brawny, midnight-haired man sits on the flowered couch next to a tiny, sparkling amber-eyed girl.

"Did you know we had a cousin?" Emilian asks. "Am I the only fucking clueless person here?"

"Language." Aunt Mirela slaps him on the head again.

"What are you talking about, moron?" the girl asks.

"This is Emilian, the obnoxious potty mouth. He's twenty-one, going on eight." Aunt Mirela rolls her eyes. "This is your cousin Nadya. She's nineteen, going on forty. And this is Fonso." She messes his hair.

"Cut it out." He swats her away.

"He's twenty-four, going on ninety."

"Whatever." Fonso stands.

"This is your cousin, Alice." She grabs my shoulders from behind pushing me forward into their tiny living room.

"When did we get a cousin?" Fonso asks. "Did

Aunt Simza adopt her?"

"Oy. No, Simza didn't adopt her. She's Lyuba's daughter. Lyuba was my younger sister who passed some time ago." She peers up at the ceiling. "Twenty-two years ago, right?"

I nod.

"Are you serious? We really have a cousin and it's not another stinkin' boy?" Nadya bounces on the couch and smiles. "Is this one of your sick jokes?"

"Trust me, I'm as surprised as y'all, but there's no denying it. She's the spitting image of her mother, rest her soul." Aunt Mirela claps her hands together. "Let's celebrate with a good Roma meal."

"Roma meal?" I ask.

"Mas." The two boys say in unison.

"Meat," Nadya explains. "It's the 'American' Roma vegetable."

"I see. Can I help?" I ask.

"There's those polite words again." Aunt Mirela beams. "Ya'll can learn a thing or two from your cousin."

Nadya jumps up, grabs my hand, and leads me to the kitchen. "Let's wash the vegetables."

"Boys." Aunt Mirela's eyebrows waggle.

"We know." Fonso heads toward the door. "We start the grill."

"I love it when we have company, but that rarely happens." Nadya hands me potatoes out of the fridge.

"It's like a miracle or something...you being our cousin and finding us." She pauses in mid stance as if a struck with a thought. "How did you find us?"

"She found Simza, who wouldn't even speak to her, for some reason. If I hadn't gone over there to make amends, I wouldn't have seen her." Aunt Mirela babbles on. "Sorry about the tomato, by the way."

"What tomato?" Nadya asks.

"I threw a tomato at her." Aunt Mirela giggles. "I thought she was the dead come to haunt me."

The tomato stain on my jeans looks like a faded blood spot.

"I can't believe you did that, Ma. Seriously, you're as crazy as a monkey on speed."

***

Nadya launches into a thousand questions, often asking one before I finish answering. I don't blame her...I had quite a few myself. I answer truthfully, for the most part. This feeling of confusion and uncertainty weighs on me.

We sit down to dinner and the harder questions start.

"Where's your pa?" Aunt Mirela asks.

My heart feels like it sinks deeper into my chest. "We parted ways a few towns ago."

"Why?" Nadya asks.

"Just time, I guess. We wanted to move to different places." I lie.

"And someone happened to send you a card with Aunt Simza's name on it?" Aunt Mirela's eyes narrow. She bites off a piece of tough French bread.

I sip my water. "Yes, that one freaked me out, but since she had the name of Mother, my curiosity was busting to be satisfied. How long have you been in town?" I try to steer the conversation in a different direction. "It's a cool place, but Cassadaga seems a bit bizarre."

"It's a perfect place for us. Mama has found more work, being closer to Cassadaga." Nadya loves to talk.

"Work?" I ask.

"She's gifted. It's in our blood," Nadya replies.

The table falls silent. Everyone looks at Nadya.

"What?" She purses her lips together. "We all want to know what her gift is, so we might as well ask. We are family, after all."

"I do past life regressions for people." Aunt Mirela continues, "It's a way to make money in a town where people travel to see psychics. I rent an office in town on the weekends."

"That's interesting." Everyone stares at me for a few moments too long. "I'm sure this is the place to do it."

"Yeah, but hers are real." Nadya says. "She allows the people to experience their lives before for themselves...as if they were there. Like they are trapped in a movie they can't escape. It's kinda creepy, to say the least."

"How would you know?" Emilian asks. "Ma won't let us do it."

"None of you are ready to learn from your past." Aunt Mirela gets up from the table and starts to clear the dishes.

"I am," Nadya whines.

"And Aunt Simza talks to the dead?" I ask.

"Yes." Fonso says. "She's probably the most talented of us all."

"She's the most talented of us all." Emilian mimics in a childish voice. "And you're the most boring of us all."

"Shut up, alien!" Nadya throws a piece of bread at him.

"No throwing of food in this house," Aunt Mirela warns. "I'll still take a switch to you. I don't care how old you are."

"He doesn't have to be so mean, Ma." Nadya sticks her tongue out at Emilian.

The sibling jealousy I felt earlier wanes. Perhaps it's best I didn't have any brothers or sisters growing up.

"Emilian, she's right. Your condescending

demeanor isn't appropriate for your age. It's time for you to act your age and respect each other. All of you. It's not like you are young kids anymore." Aunt Mirela takes my plate.

"Thank you," I say. "What do you do, Fonso?"

"Nothing." Emilian says. "The gift skipped him. He's probably the mailman's kid or something. With that jet-black hair, he doesn't look Rom to me."

"Emilian, out!" Aunt Mirela points toward the hallway.

Emilian scrapes his chair against the linoleum floor, turns, and stomps off toward his room.

Fonso, who's sitting next to me, places his hands on the table and balls them into fists.

I grab his left hand and squeeze. "Don't worry. The gift skipped me, too."

His expression softens as he gazes into my eyes, studying me. His mouth turns into a half-smile. "I knew I'd like you."

"Doesn't anyone want to know my gift?" Nadya asks.

"Of course," I reply.

She beams. "I can find anyone or anything just by thinking about it."

"Yeah, she's a real bore at hide and seek." Fonso laughs.

"It comes in handy." Nadya looks at Aunt Mirela.

"Absolutely." Aunt Mirela says. "I never lose my

car keys anymore."

"Yes, you do!" Fonso says, "Now, you just have your crazy daughter find them for you."

We all laugh and the air around us feels lighter.

"Too bad you don't have a gift." Nadya twirls her hair around her finger. "I think our line is dwindling with gifts, huh Ma?"

"Maybe." Aunt Mirela starts washing the dishes.

"What's Emilian's gift?" I ask.

"Oh, Emilian...he sees people for what they really are," Nadya explains.

"Like what?" A nervousness grows in my stomach, wondering if he saw through my lies.

Nadya replies, "You know... vampires, witches, and stuff. There's a pack of werewolves living down the street."

CHAPTER 7

LEARNING ABOUT MY family's abilities is one thing, but hearing them talk about vampires, witches, and werewolves existing in society is another. This unexpected mini-reunion just took a turn for the worst.

"Thank you so much for lunch. It was fabulous." I stand and take the rest of the dishes on the table into the kitchen. "I need to get into town and look for a job. Is there a bus stop near?"

"I'll take you." Fonso offers. "I was heading to the bookstore anyway."

"Really? That would be great."

"Can I come?" Nadya asks. "There's nothing to do here and I can show you around."

I reluctantly nod. "Okay." My aching desire to be alone is suddenly squashed.

She claps her hands. "Give me a minute to get my

purse." She runs down the hallway.

"You aren't going to go all introvert on us, are you?" Aunt Mirela asks.

"No, not at all. I just found out I have a family." I smile, and think about the reason I'm here. I need to find out what happened to Dad. I would love their help, especially Nadya's, but I don't know if I can trust my new found family yet. "You won't get rid of me that easily."

"Good." Aunt Mirela hugs me. "Come by real soon, please. We have so much to catch up on."

"Okay." I follow Fonso toward the door.

"We're leaving Nadya!" Fonso yells.

"Coming!" Nadya's voice echoes in the small home. She runs down the hall. "I'm ready."

"Don't stay out too late." Aunt Mirela shakes a finger at them.

"Yeah, the bookstore stays open real late, Ma." Fonso's sarcastic sense of humor cracks me up. "Did it occur to you that we are all over the age of 18, with most of us being over the drinking age? Heck, Alice here is younger than me and all on her own."

"Do you want me to switch you for back talking me?" Aunt Mirela asks.

"No Mam." Fonso rushes out the door and we follow.

***

LIGHTNING STRUCK

Nadya talks the entire 15 minutes during the car ride to town, telling me about her boring childhood, having to be homeschooled, and never getting out much. Luckily, the road the campground is on is the same road to town, so getting home won't be difficult.

"I'm going to do what you did, Alice." Nadya's head bobs a few times.

"What's that?" I ask.

"Go my own way." She waves her hand and arm. "Be independent and free."

"You'd survive all of two seconds." Fonso chuckles. "You need money to survive, Sis, and that means a job."

"Well, poop." Nadya crosses her arms and pouts.

"Meet me by the fountain in an hour or two?" Fonso asks Nadya.

"Ya, make it two."

"Thank you for the ride. I think I can make it home from here." I pat the map to be sure it's still in my pocket.

"Where are you staying?" Fonso asks.

"At the campground where Aunt Simza lives...in a cabin there."

"I don't mind giving you a ride back to your cabin." Fonso offers.

I shake my head. "I'll be fine. I may need some time to unwind and process this day."

"Oh, I understand." He parks the car next to a curb. Taking a pen and scratch paper out of the glove box, he hands me his number. "Call me if you need me."

"Don't you forget me, Fonso." Nadya says. "I'll be waiting at the fountain in two hours."

"Who could possibly forget you?" He smirks and drives away.

"I wish I'd had a sister." She sighs.

"Do you know of anywhere that's hiring?" The town looks small and quaint, out of a Thomas Kindcade painting. Small shops line the town square, with a circular fountain in the middle surrounded by one large, brick roundabout. "It looks so calm here."

"Nothing compared to Baton Rouge, I suppose." Nadya nudges me. "Let's walk around and see if there isn't something for you."

"What about you?" I inquire. "No job?"

"Working isn't for me. Not much use for someone to locate things."

"What about becoming a detective? Surely you'd find all the clues to the case." We pass a coffee shop and the dark, coffee bean aroma drifts out the open door. I'm tempted to order a cup, but maybe I'll do that later when I'm alone and can sit and think for a while.

"Doesn't interest me much, although I could be great at missing persons cases. I've heard some psychics help out on cases from time-to-time and I bet they make good money at it. Don't ya think?"

"Makes sense to me, since they offer rewards." We continue past a women's clothing store with one elderly clerk. She glances up from the magazine at us. By the frown on her face, I don't think they would hire me there. "How about finding me a job, if you're so good at finding things?"

"That'd be a first for me. I've never tried finding something like that." She stops and closes her eyes.

"I was only kidding." I giggle.

"Shhh, give me a second." She clasps her hands together and squeezes them tight. "Go right at the next intersection and walk straight for a few blocks."

"Okay." She opens her eyes, grabs my hand, and we rush down the sidewalk toward the intersection.

"A little bit of faith, dear cousin, goes a long way."

We head down the street. I survey it as best I can. There is a real estate office, a small hardware store, and a Chinese food restaurant that appears to cater mostly to take-out. It's refreshing not being surrounded by large corporate discount stores.

We pass an alleyway that runs behind the shops. I bump into Nadya when she stops short. "There." She points to a diner on the opposite corner across the street with a red and white 'Help Wanted' sign on the window.

"Okay, that's amazing. How the heck..." I'm dumbfounded.

"Another service I'm good for." She beams. "Let's go in and ask about it."

"Do you know anyone that works there?"

"Nope. We don't eat in town much." She starts across the empty two-way street.

A few cars line the small parking lot on the side of the diner. An old-fashioned bell tied to the top of the door dings as Nadya enters.

"Where are my keys?" a big burly man hollers through the kitchen.

An elderly woman stands behind a cash register. "May I help you?"

"I'm inquiring about the 'Help Wanted' sign." I point toward the window. "What are you hiring for?"

Nadya moves to the side looking at the brochure stand.

"Are you from around here?" the old woman asks.

"I just moved into town, staying near Cassadaga." I fake a half-smile.

"I asked where my keys are." The heavy-set man draped in a white apron smeared with food grease comes around the corner.

"Well, I don't know where you left them," the cranky cashier says. "It's not my job."

"What have we here?" He scratches the stubble

on his chin and grins at me. He's missing one of his top teeth. "Are you here for the job?"

"She's not from around here." She crosses her arms.

"If I find your keys, will you hire my cousin?" Nadya says.

The man looks at her and at me. "Have you ever waited tables?"

I look around the small diner and see it only seats maybe 50 people. I've worked at busier establishments. "Always."

He turns to Nadya. "Okay, find my keys and she has a job."

"But—" the old lady says.

"But, nothing, you old hag." He pushes his back against her. "So, where are my keys."

Nadya skips past the counter, opens a draw opposite the cash register, and pulls out a string of keys.

"I'll be damned." He scratches his head. "How'd you do that?"

"It's kooky, if you ask me," the old lady says.

"Lucky, I guess." Nadya prances away.

"Huh. Well, I'm Roger and this old bag is Abby." He points his thumb in the air toward her. "Oh, and there's Kyle in the back. Kyle!" He hollers toward the kitchen.

A topaz-eyed, tousled wheat-haired impressive

looking man pops his head out the window.

"Yeah?" Kyle looks at Roger.

"That's Kyle." Roger points to him. "He cooks from time to time...when he's not out surfing and goofing around."

Kyle's glittering eyes meet mine. He smiles. I see a depth in his eyes...it's screaming to be exposed and understood. In that moment, the noise around us fades into low static.

"Earth to, what is her name?" Roger breaks my concentration.

"Alice. Her name's Alice," Nadya replies.

A flush creeps up my face. "Yes, sorry, it's Alice Murphy."

"Every single time." Roger rolls his eyes and stares at Abby. "He always gets that same damn reaction."

Nadya twinkles her fingers at Kyle. He grins and backs up, hitting his head on the metal rolling rack that holds the orders.

"Can you start tonight?" Roger asks.

"Yes. What time?"

"Be here by five for the evening shift." Roger pats Abby on the back. "Abby can show you the ropes.

"Gladly." Abby's mouth sets in a hard line.

"Great. Thank you." I hold my hand out and Roger grabs it firmly. "See you later."

LIGHTNING STRUCK

Nadya holds the door open for me. I glance over my shoulder toward the kitchen and see Kyle watching me.

"This is like one of the best days ever," Nadya says. "I mean, you come to town and we have a real cousin, you find a job right away, and we now know where the sexiest man in town works. I'll be stalking him all the time." She looks through the diner window. "I need to turn my radar to find more hot guys."

"Thank you." I nudge her forward down the sidewalk.

"I should be thanking you." She stops at the corner of the diner where no one inside can see us. "But, he was eyeing you the entire time. I don't even think he realized I was in the room."

"That's not true. He was just being nice since they hired me." Part of me wants Nadya's statement to be true, but I'm sure a guy like that has a string of girlfriends in line. Heck, he's probably got a waiting list.

"Either you're blind or in denial. He even smacked his head." She grabs her head to demonstrate. "He couldn't take his eyes off you."

"Well, it's too bad we'll be working together, because you can't date people you work with."

"Says who?" One of her eyebrows arch. "If you don't want him I call dibs."

"You don't have a boyfriend? You're beautiful! I'm sure some guy will grab you up soon."

"Yeah, right. Have you met my family? They're a bunch of loons. Besides, Ma wouldn't go for it. She says it would dilute our genes to date anyone who wasn't Roma." She frowns.

"Are you serious?"

She nods.

"Are there Roma families around other than yours—I mean ours?"

"Not that I know of. We haven't traveled with our kind for a long time now. Ma said it was too dangerous, but never really said much more. I think she was spurned by love. Pa drank a lot and Ma had enough, so she left him with his family and we never looked back."

"I'm sorry, I didn't know." I walk down the street and step in front of the alleyway.

A huge, lifted truck barrels through the alley...the alley I just stepped in front of.

CHAPTER 8

HANDS GRAB MY shoulders and pull me back. I fall into a heavy pair of arms and look up into my topaz-eyed savior: Kyle. My heart races a mile per minute. Screeching, the truck stops a few feet from me. He pushes me upward on my feet. Nadya's hands cover her mouth as she backs against the brick wall of the building.

"Are you crazy?" Kyle yells at the truck driver.

The tinted windows on the driver's door, and the door behind it, lower.

"Why the hell were you speeding down the damn alleyway? You could have killed someone and almost did." Kyle points at me.

The driver turns his head slowly, as if it's an inconvenience to notice to us. He sweeps his tawny-brown shoulder-length hair from his face, revealing his rugged short facial hair. He glares at Kyle and eyes me.

A stocky guy, in the backseat, forms an odd-twisted grin, his eyes moving back and forth from Kyle to the driver. A girl in the front seat next to the driver glares at me while chomping on gum as if I'm the rude party in this bizarre encounter.

"It's all right," Nadya comforts Kyle with her hands, while slowly edging him further away from the truck. She jerks her head to the side, motioning me to move back. "No harm done."

"Bullshit!" Kyle brushes her away. "He's a fucking selfish asshole. He's not even apologizing."

The truck driver's stare doesn't leave me and he still doesn't say one word.

The girl in the front seat shoves the driver. "Let's go, Colin."

The windows roll back up, but Colin's gaze follows me.

"Let's get out of here, Alice," Nadya pleads. "Let's go shopping before you need to work."

"Shopping?" I break eye contact. The truck turns left, racing down the street.

"Are you okay?" Kyle asks.

"I'm fine, thank you."

"Yes, thank you hunky Kyle." Nadya pushes me forward. "We have to get going so we have time to shop before Alice has to work."

"See you later." Kyle waves, walking to the rear of the diner.

"What was that about?" I ask.

"Do you remember when we were talking about what Emilian's ability was?"

I nod.

"Remember when I said there was a pack of werewolves living in town?"

I stop on the sidewalk in front of a vacant office space. "You mean the people in the truck are werewolves?" I laugh. I can't help it.

"That's Colin Moore. He's like their leader or alpha or something. Laugh all you want, but I'm telling you to stay away from them." Nadya walks ahead of me.

I jog to keep up. "Sorry, but it sounds ridiculous." I regret the words as soon as they leave my mouth and a tinge of guilt forms.

"You don't believe?" Nadya asks. "In all your life, you've never run across a nightwalker or shifter?"

"I can't say I have. It's imaginary stuff."

"It's nightmare stuff. We can't seem to lose them." Nadya presses the crosswalk button. A few people throw coins into the fountain in the center of town.

"What do you mean?" I ask.

"Everywhere we move, and we move often, there always seems to be a pack in town. It's like they are everywhere, infesting every town."

"Werewolves?" I ask. "Have you ever seen someone change into a wolf?"

"Well, no."

"But, you're sure they exist and you trust your brother's word?" I ask.

She faces me with a serious expression. "Alice, you have to trust family. They're all you have sometimes."

I remain quiet, thinking about Dad. I've always relied on his guidance and ability. When he said move, we moved. When he told me about the Hunters, I believed him...believe him. I saw them with my own eyes, chasing me, like he always warned me. They want us dead.

"Fonso is here." Nadya looks across the fountain, watching Fonso reading on a bench. "I guess our shopping trip will have to wait."

"Are you angry with me?" I ask.

She shakes her head. "No. I'm mentally worn out from the day."

"Thank you again for helping me with the job." I hug her.

"Do you mind if I visit you at your place sometime? It's nice to get away from the house once in a while."

"Sure. Any time."

She rushes across the street. She and Fonso wave.

Had she stayed a moment longer, I might have

asked about the Hunters. Surely, if she believes in vampires and werewolves, she might know something of the Hunters.

I have an hour before work so I decide to buy a tea at the coffee shop. I sit outdoors to soak in a few rays of light before the darkness creeps up. A bus comes to a stop...the stop that I'll take home later. It lingers on the edge of town, on the road that runs straight to the campground. This is probably one of the less complicated towns I've ever stayed in.

The day's events swarm through my head the instant I sit at the pewter table. Nadya's belief Colin and his friends are werewolves seems so strong it's almost believable. All of my cousin's stated abilities, with the exception of Fonso, makes me think about Dad and his gift. He always knew when we needed to leave...when we were found by the Hunters. Nadya did seem great at finding things...the keys, the job. She has me believing in her hidden talent. Perhaps she can locate Dad for me. That would mean I'd need to confide in her with my purpose for being here. I'd have to tell the truth...my real story.

***

Five o'clock nears and I'm nervous. It's always scary starting at new job in a new place, but now I'll be dealing with a gorgeous Kyle on top of it. Some of the shops start closing as I walk toward the diner. The coffee shop stays open late, as well as the tiny theater across the road.

Before I cross the street, a loud engine revs near me. It's the tinted monster truck from earlier. It intentionally creeps up next to me. I pick up my pace and it moves forward, matching my step. He's toying with me.

I back up and run behind it to the other side of the street. Colin rolls down his window. He's alone this time.

"What?" I wait for the reply that doesn't come.

Colin's hair covers the side of his face, but I see him staring at me.

He revs his engine and takes off.

The diner bell is a welcome sound.

"Hello," I greet Abby, who leans against the back counter.

"Here you are." Abby reaches into a drawer and pulls out a ticket pad and pen. "Write down what they want and put it on that silver circular thing there." She points toward the kitchen window. "If you get bored, tidy up behind the counter—that's your station, too. And we don't have no busboy to clean tables either, so that duty falls on you."

"Got it." I take the pad and pen from her. "Are there any other waitresses?"

"We have two girls who handle breakfast, but

you'll be our night waitress. We always have a hard time keeping someone for that shift." Abby leans back against the counter.

"Why is that?"

She shrugs.

"Okay." I walk around the counter to my new post, surveying what I'm dealing with. There's a drink and salad station. It's all relatively simple.

"She's a bunch of fun, isn't she?" Kyle says from the kitchen. He smiles and nods toward Abby.

"Yeah."

"It's slow, but it'll pick up soon." Kyle dries his hands with a cloth. "If you have any questions, feel free to ask me."

"Thanks."

I study the menu. Customers roll in. For the next five hours, business stays steady, and our only conversations center around the food orders.

Abby leaves at 10:00PM, placing me in charge of cashing out the guests on top of serving them. The last hour drags since only a few hungry customers stagger in and out. Most of the patrons are younger and talk about a movie they watched at the theater.

Roger walks in from the back. I didn't see him the entire evening. "How was your first night?"

"It went well." I place my pen and pad into the drawer. "It was busy for a while, but I managed."

"Excellent." Roger turns the 'open' sign off and

locks the door. "Seems like you cleaned up the tables and behind the counter pretty good."

"Thank you." I take off the borrowed apron and place it on the hook against the wall.

"Now, we didn't talk about pay or anything, and I'm sure you are anxious to get on your way, but are you agreeable to working five evenings per week at a flat rate of two hundred dollars cash plus tips?" Roger scratches his chin. "This way we don't need to do all that nasty paperwork. I got two women for the morning shifts, but you would be our main night server. Abby will take the other two nights."

"Roger, that sounds great to me." I hold out my hand.

He smiles and shakes it. "Alice, I think this will work out fine."

He opens the cash register and starts placing the cash into a deposit bag.

"I'll come in about this time every night and close out so you can head on home." Roger shuts the register. "See you tomorrow."

"See you tomorrow." I head toward the front door. Roger follows behind.

"Wait, I'm coming." Kyle pops out from the kitchen. "Back door is locked Roger, and Felipe is finishing up the dishes."

"Thanks Kyle. See ya." Roger locks the door behind us.

"What did you think?" Kyle asks.

"It's a cute diner. Roger seems nice." I scratch my sore shoulder, recalling lugging my duffel bag around in New Orleans.

"Yeah, it's a laid back place. I think that's what I like about it."

"How long have you worked here?"

"Not long. Only a few months." Kyle points to a Jeep. "Do you need a lift home?"

"No, that's okay."

"Are you sure? It's no trouble." He smiles.

"Thank you, but I prefer to walk to wind down." I wave and walk toward town.

"Bye Alice." Kyle waves.

I glance back when I'm across the street and see him watching me. I wave again before I turn the corner. The coffee shop is closed and the theater is dark. I guess they don't have late hours here.

The light above the bus stop is out. A tall, looming figure leans against the glass. It's Colin.

CHAPTER 9

"**D**O YOU KNOW how long I've been waiting for you?" Colin asks.

"Let me guess...your entire life?" I give him a half-fake smile. "Where's your big truck? You want to try to run me over again?"

A minor electric feeling passes through me the closer I move toward Colin.

He smiles, revealing gleaming white teeth. He's taller than I imagined, standing at least 6'3" with a muscular barrel-chest. He sports a nice tan, which is slightly darker than my olive complexion. "I formally apologize for nearly running you over earlier, my lady." He bows.

"Was that so hard?" I sit on the bench. "Apologizing, that is. Maybe you didn't want to appear weak in front of your friends. You just stared and said nothing."

I watch the tree lines across the street, trying to

appear uninterested, but all I want to do is turn and study him. This feeling...it's as if he were a magnet and I was iron...I'm drawn to him.

"I was so mesmerized by you that words didn't seem appropriate at the time." He sits next to me. "I'm Colin Moore, by the way."

"Yes, I've...my cousin, Nadya told me." I peek at him through my hair.

"Nadya is your cousin?" His voice crackles a little. He clears his throat.

I nod. "Do you know her?"

"They live down the street." He points toward the darkened road. "We let her brother hang with us sometimes. He's kind of our mascot." He chuckles. "Are you adopted?"

I look him straight in the eyes. "I'm not adopted. What kind of question is that?"

He shrugs. "I suppose I don't see the family resemblance."

"Wait, how did you know I'd be coming to the bus stop? Have you been watching me?"

"I saw you in the diner and I didn't see you driving, so I assumed you'd take the bus after work. You're late though. The last bus took off fifteen minutes ago."

I look up and down the road. "Really?"

"Last bus leaves at eleven."

"Damn." I look at my watch.

"But, it's your lucky night. I'm your knight in shining armor." He holds his arms up and I visualize him beating his chest like Tarzan...I need to reign in my imagination.

"I, umm...I can walk." I mumble, and stand. "It's not too far." I hope.

"You don't sound too sure. When did you get into town?"

"Last night."

"You never told me your name." He stands, facing me.

"I didn't?" Why am I so flustered around him? "It's El... Alice."

"You sure that's your name?" He laughs.

"I think I know my own name. It's Alice." I purse my lips, more angry with myself.

"Alice doesn't sound like a Rom name. And you're related to the Kepi clan?"

"How did...how do you know their last name and why call them a clan? What's that supposed to mean?"

"Why are you so easily offended?" he asks. "I told you Emilian hangs with us. We know the family."

"We, meaning your clan?" I cross my arms. "Does your clan start with a Klu and a Klux?"

He stares into my eyes and although I want to stay angry with him, my resolve melts as if the rain

72

washes it down the drain.

"Come with me. The night's young." He holds his hand out.

Not taking my eyes from his, I slide my fingers into his hand and a static shock runs through my body. Even though I'm sure he felt it, he doesn't flinch.

Wrapping my fingers in with his, he leads me to his truck.

"Where are we going?" He opens the door. I'm instantly flustered as to how I'm supposed to hoist myself up that far. He grabs my waist from behind. The smell of an oceanic musk drifts up my nostrils and I want to press back into him, but I stiffen. He lifts me as if I'm as light as a doll, and places me on the running board. I climb into the cab and put on my seatbelt.

"I'm not sure yet, but might as well get to know each other better before I bring you home." He winks and shuts the door.

This day is not turning out the way I thought it would. First, a family I don't quite know how to explain, then a job with the dreamy Kyle and now this...what is this? I'm accepting rides from a perfect stranger who tried to run me over but I'm so incredibly drawn to...and who Nadya thinks is a...werewolf. I'm suddenly mentally exhausted and my head throbs.

"Colin, do you mind taking me home? I'm tired from a rather crazy day and I don't think I can take any more surprises."

He nods. "Where do you live? Are you staying with your cousins?"

"No, I'm at this campground down the street." I close my eyes and place my palm against my forehead. "I can show you."

"The one where your other aunt lives? Or is that your mom?"

He knows a lot more than I thought. "It's my aunt, too, and yes, that's the one. I'm staying in a cabin."

He starts the engine. "That's rustic. I like it."

"I wouldn't call it rustic, but it's a nice little place." The deal Deena made with me is extremely lucky. Dad would like it.

"Where did you move from?" He turns onto the darkened road leading to the campground.

"Louisiana." My chest aches and a slow rain falls.

The windshield wipers screech across the window. "I guess it's probably not a good night to be out after all."

"Guess not." My emotions take a turn for the worse as the thought of Dad weighs on my mind. That Hunter who showed up in New Orleans said she would take me to him. Does that mean he's still alive? Are they using him to find me? Many unanswered questions float through my head.

"Which cabin?"

"Huh?" I squint out the watery windows to see we are at the campground. "Oh, it's the first one there." I point.

He parks in front of the cabin. "Do you work tomorrow?"

"Yes, but not until five o'clock." I gaze into his obsidian eyes. "I'm working the late shift there five days a week." God, why the hell am I being so forthcoming with answers with this guy? I unbuckle the seat belt wanting to get out before I say something I'd regret.

"That's cool." His hands grip the steering wheel. "Spend the day with me tomorrow?"

"What?"

"I'll be here at eight in the morning."

"Colin, may I ask you something strange?" I bite my lower lip.

He turns toward me.

"Are you—do you live around here?" I couldn't ask what I wanted to. It sounds too stupid in my head to say aloud. *Colin, are you a werewolf?* Yes, excessively stupid.

"Yes, that is a mighty strange question. It's probably one of the most bizarre questions I've ever been asked." He laughs and I join in.

Not as strange as what I really want to ask you.

"I live about ten minutes east of here." He grins. "Is that all you wanted to ask me?"

"Yes...for now." I touch the door handle. The rain lightens. "I'll see you tomorrow." I don't know why I agree to spend the day with him, but something tells me I'm not the only one in for any surprises.

"Alice?"

I turn back toward him. "Hmm?"

"Don't tell anyone else you're Rom or related to the Kepi family for now. Let's keep it between us."

"Why?"

"They are a bizarre group and people around here are judgmental. I wouldn't want anyone getting the wrong impression of you." He shrugs.

"I learned a long time ago to not care what anyone thinks of me." A smidge of irritation courses through me. "And if you want to be my friend I'm sure you wouldn't care what others think of me either, would you?"

The thunder rolls in.

"I would never." His hands cross over his heart. He grabs my left hand and pulls it up. "But, it's not always safe for the Roma here...even in a town where strange is accepted."

He kisses my hand and jumps into the drizzling shower. He rushes around to my side and opens my door.

Helping me down, he pulls me close to him. My

body slides down his as he sets me on the ground; our faces are only inches apart.

"Till tomorrow." He pulls away and rushes back to the driver's side door, leaving me breathless.

His truck pulls out of the campground. I stand on my small porch. *It's not always safe for the Roma...*Was he warning me?

CHAPTER 10

BUTTERFLIES TICKLE MY stomach when he knocks on the door; instead of Colin standing to greet me at the cabin door, it's Kyle.

"Hi." I force a smile.

"I ran into your cousin this morning getting coffee. She told me where you were staying." He runs his hand through his hair, pushing some stray hairs back. "I was wondering if you'd like to get breakfast, but I see you have plans." He looks at Colin grinning as he leans against his truck.

"I...umm...we ran into each other last night. I think he's trying to make up for almost killing me yesterday." I fumble through the explanation, wringing my fingers. "He's trying to be nice by showing me around, since I'm new to town."

"Colin and nice don't go together." His brows lift. "Alice, please be careful." He opens his mouth as if he wants to go on, but he presses his lips together.

"I will. See you later at the diner?"

He nods. "See ya."

The guys exchange passing glares as Kyle walks to his Jeep, but neither of them says a word. Kyle's Jeep's tires throw up dirt as it takes off, bringing a cloud of dust toward Colin's truck.

Day two in Cassadaga and things are already becoming complicated.

"Look at you...already making friends." Colin smirks. "Should we have invited him out with us?"

I lock the cabin up. "You're not funny."

"And you're gorgeous." Colin stands close to me when I turn around. My breath catches in my throat. He brushes my hair behind my right ear. "How about seeing the Atlantic today?"

Breathe Elysia. "The beach?" I exhale. "I don't have a bathing suit."

"You move to Florida without owning a bathing suit?" He smiles. "We will have to rectify this situation."

He grabs my hand and leads me to his truck.

Glancing down the street, I notice Aunt Simza watching us through a window. When she sees me, she quickly closes the curtain.

Deena waves as we pass the campground storefront.

"How do you know Kyle?" I ask.

"Huh?"

"It seems as if you two know each other." The passing trees lining the street become a green blur. "You don't seem to like each other either."

"I guess you can say we were schooled together, and you're right, we don't see eye-to-eye."

"Schooled together?"

His eyes stay on the road.

"Did you go to school together?" I recall the way his passenger kept watching their exchange yesterday.

"We hung out in different circles." Colin wets his lips. "He never liked my friends and I'm not particularly fond of his."

"I see." A gut feeling itches at me...he's not completely forthcoming with information. It's not often these feelings come over me, but when they do it's bothersome. They'll drive me nuts until I squeeze every last drop from him.

"There's a little shop close to the beach that sells bikinis." The corner of his mouth lifts. "It'll be fun seeing you try them on."

"What makes you think I'm a bikini girl? Maybe I'm a one-piece, cover-up type." I'm definitely a bikini girl. I have...had this adorable purple and blue stripped bikini. Will he notice I only have three outfits? This part of moving and starting over sucks. I should be out shopping and rebuilding my life, not jetting off to the beach with a mysterious guy.

"I'm sure you're a bikini girl." He winks.

A short twenty-minute ride and I see the blue ocean with not a cloud in sight. The small waves crash against the coppery shore. It's different from the whiter sand at Panama Beach.

The swimsuit store isn't far from the shore. Colin parks his truck in two spots, backing in so its tail isn't sticking out in traffic. While he pays at a meter station, I close my eyes and listen to the sounds of the waves hitting the sand mixed with the seagulls squawks and the occasional passing car.

"Daydreaming?" Colin stirs my thoughts.

"Making memories through the sounds." We cross the street. "You should try it some time."

"Yeah, that's real manly." He rolls his shoulders, pressing his chest out. "Did you mistake me for a metrosexual?"

"Heavens, no. I would never."

He whirls me to face him, bringing me close to him and his natural, musky scent. "Good, because my ego would be bruised if you had."

"Big truck, rugged look...not screaming metrosexual. But..." I haw.

"But what?"

"Your metrosexual side could be hiding in a closet, screaming to get out." I run my hand down his chest, giving him a pat. "It's been known to happen."

He leans closer to my ear, his breath tickling my neck, sending shivers through me. "I don't think it'll happen today," he whispers. He pulls back. "Here we are."

Disappointment bubbles within me. Each time he gets close I think he'll lean in and kiss me. Each time he doesn't and I'm filled with disappointment. *Seriously, what is wrong with me? I just met this guy and already I want to—* I cut off the distracting thought as I walk into the bikini shop. It is glorious. There must be a million suits hanging on racks throughout and against the wall, they go all the way up to the ceiling, every color, pattern, and style.

"Unbelievable. I thought you said it was a little shop?"

He smiles. I browse, picking up a bathing suit here and there, as he follows me around. Once I gather enough, he sits in a cushiony seat while I try them on in the dressing room.

"Aren't you going to show me?" he hollers.

"No."

"What's the point of me bringing you bikini shopping if I can't see the merchandise?" He laughs.

"Fine." I open the door to show him the first one. He nods with each subsequent suit I try on. "What's the point of having your opinion when you approve of each one?"

"Maybe you should buy them all and change

every fifteen minutes for me." He laughs. "I like the teal, polka-dotted one."

"Me, too." I admire it in the mirror before taking it off. "And, I'm only buying one."

The price is as much as my groceries would cost for two weeks. My stomach growls realizing I haven't eaten.

"I'm going to the truck to get the blanket and towels. Meet you out front."

"Okay."

He's out of the store by the time I change and leave the dressing room. After putting the others back and deciding on the teal one, I dig out my money at the register.

"It's already paid for." The cashier unclips the security device and places the suit in their paper-handled bag.

"Excuse me?"

"Your boyfriend paid for it before he left." She smiles. "Have a great day."

My boyfriend? "Thank you." I take the bag, half relieved and half infuriated. "Can I change in here?"

"Sure thing."

I hurry back to put my bikini on under my jeans, thinking about the expensive gift Colin bought me. Why did he do that?

He sits on a bench next to a basket, a blanket, and a couple of towels.

"You didn't have to buy me the bikini. I could've bought it myself."

"I know." He picks up everything. "All you have to do is say thank you."

"Thank you." I follow him.

"You're welcome."

"What's in the basket?"

We walk next to each other, down a sand bank lined with wild looking plants I've never seen before. It's impossible to keep the sand from getting in my sandals.

"It's a surprise."

I follow him further down the beach until we hit a cozy alcove surrounded by plants. The few people here are further north, giving us more privacy. I'm not sure if this is a good thing or not. "This is nice."

Colin spreads the blanket out and places the basket to the side. He takes off his shirt, revealing chiseled, slightly hairy chest. "See something you like?"

I avert my eyes and look toward the sea. "Yes, the ocean is quite lovely."

"Are you going to wear your jeans all day?" He stretches on the blanket, making it harder and harder to concentrate on anything else but his body.

His aqua blue swim shorts complement my bikini...the bikini hiding under my jeans and tank top. All of a sudden, a self-conscious feeling erupts inside me, making me feel unworthy of his companionship. He belongs on a *GQ* cover and I belong on the pages of a Tampax ad.

"Come into the water with me?" I peel off my jeans and toss my tank top on the blanket. "I've never been in the Atlantic."

"Is that a fact?" He rises. "Then let's go."

Colin grabs my hand. We run down to the shore. The water feels icy. He lifts me out of the cold, pulling me to his bare chest and falls back into the incoming wave.

Blinking away the soft salt sting, I splash him and swim further into the shallow depths of the ocean. His hands find my waist and stop me from swimming out farther.

"Where are you going?" He pulls me to him. "Trying to escape my evil clutches?"

We stare into each other's eyes for what feels like an eternity, neither saying a word. Our bodies move up and down with the flow of waves as if we are one with the water. The sounds dissolve and there's nothing and no one but us. It's the most intimate moment I've ever shared with anyone...it's the perfect time for that first kiss.

Out of the corner of my eye I spy a white raindrop, falling fast. It lands on his head and drips down his face.

"Colin, I think a bird pooped on your head." His

lips curl into a smile and he laughs. He splashes at the sky, missing the bird that's flying too high.

"He's laughing at me." Colin dives underwater to erase all evidence of the bombing. "That was probably the least romantic attempt ever."

"That seagull had it in for you, no doubt."

"Are you hungry?" he asks. "I'm feeling like chicken about now. You hear that, bird? I'm going to eat your friend."

"I'm starving."

The sand clings to my wet feet as we make our way back to the blanket.

Colin opens the picnic basket to reveal chips, fried chicken, and a container of fruit. "I didn't know what you would like." He tilts it to offer me first choice.

"I'll take some...all of it please."

"A woman after my own heart."

"Look who's here." A strange, deep feminine voice booms.

"Jesus." Colin mutters.

Blocking the sun with my hand, I see Colin's friends standing over us with my cousin, Emilian.

"What's going on?" A gangly guy asks. He flops down between us, grabbing a piece of chicken out of Colin's hand. "Well, hello to you. I'm Brayden. That's Riley and Kayla." He tears into the meat and winks at me.

"Yeah, what's going on Colin?" The girl, my age, stands with her hands on her hips, eyeing Colin and me.

"Kayla, don't start." Colin rises.

"Start what?" she asks. "I don't start nothing, but I'll sure as hell finish it." She glares at me and growls.

She actually growls at me.

"Kayla, back off," Colin commands.

"Hey cuz." Emilian helps me up.

"Cuz?" Kayla's jaw drops. "She's a fucking Rom, Colin? Really?"

Heat rises within me. "What did you call me?"

"You heard me, you Roma bitch!" Kayla steps toward me.

"Enough, Kayla." Colin pushes her back, blocking her from me.

"You don't even know me, you cow!" I yell. Thunder booms in the approaching gray clouds.

"Oh no," Brayden says.

Kayla shoves Colin out of the way and lunges for me.

Adrenaline courses through my body. I move to the side, grabbing her ponytail and thrusting her into the sand.

The gray clouds turn charcoal.

Kayla grabs my ankle and yanks me down, sucker punching me in my side.

The back of my hand connects with her face.

Strong arms pull me away from Kayla.

The clouds rage with darkness and lightning dances in the sky. Its path becomes clear. That bolt will strike the object of my anger. Kayla's doomed.

CHAPTER 11

BRAYDEN PLOWS INTO Kayla, pushing her out of the lightning bolt's path. The blinding light spreads outward for less than a second. Brayden and Kayla close their eyes and duck away, instinct driving them to take cover from its power. A booming crack follows moments after it strikes the sand, causing everyone to grab their ears...everyone but me.

Arms encircle me, pulling me further from the glowing embers emanating from the spot in the sand the bolt hit. Colin holds me. A calmness overcomes me as his hand moves over the rear of my head and continues downward, caressing my back. That's never happened to me before.

Dad's comfort in times of distress never calmed me in this way.

The charcoal clouds lighten and disperse over the area, making way for the return of the blueness we saw when we first arrived.

"Did you see that?" Emilian's bulging eyes dash from the strike site to Riley, who's helping Brayden with a shaking Kayla.

"No, you birdbrain. We didn't see the damn lightning bolt right in front of our fuckin' eyes." Brayden gazes at the gray sand where it struck.

The wet sand pulls inward, making it look like a giant spider formation with many legs sticking out of the center. A shiny tinkle glistens at its core.

"I've got to go." I push away from Colin, grabbing my bag, jeans, and tank.

"What? Are you okay?" Colin asks.

Kayla stares at me. She says nothing. For a moment, her eyes tell me she knows.

"I have to go." I repeat and take off down the sand.

"Wait!" Colin calls after me, but I'm already at the walkway leading toward the boardwalk. I don't look back.

I run north, toward the shops lining the streets. I enter the first one I come to, a bait and tackle store. "Hi." My rapid breathing slows. "May I borrow your phone?"

The clerk hands me his cell phone. I dig the number out of my bag and call the only person I know to call.

"Fonso, it's Alice. Can you come get me?"

LIGHTNING STRUCK

He agrees. I ask the clerk where I am and tell Fonso.

After putting my clothes on, I sit on a bench under a tall palm tree outside the bait store. Crossing my legs, I clear my mind to meditate, but the events play over in my head and it's hard to banish them.

Breathe, Elysia. Dad's advice plays over and over, like a broken record player. *Think of a good thought...a good memory.*

A few months ago, Lalya, a girl I worked with, surprised me with a cake. She made all the other wait staff sing to me as we often sang to the customers. It wasn't a cheap cake that one picks up at the store. It was a decorative cake like those found in expensive bakeries. She had them put two dolphins on top. It was almost too pretty to eat.

That was a good day. She was an amazing friend...one of many I've left over the years and will never see again.

Breathe Elysia.

In the distance, the waves crash against the shore. An image of dolphins pops into my head. They are super intelligent animals...at least that's what I read. They are beautiful and graceful. I'd watch them for hours on the beach when I was younger. They'd play in groups and jump out of the water. Those were good days, too.

"A penny for your thoughts?" Fonso sits next to

me. "I got here as soon as I could."

I hug him.

"What was that for?" he asks.

"Thank you for coming to get me."

"No problem. What happened?"

"Another bad mistake on my part, I'm sure."

"Let me guess." He grabs my hand, pulling me off the bench and weaves my arm through his. "Jealous ex-girlfriend ruins perfectly good picnic?"

My mouth falls open.

He laughs. "No, I'm not psychic. Emilian called me a few minutes after you did and told me all the juicy details."

"She's an ex-girlfriend, huh?"

"Apparently." He opens his car door for me. "I don't hang around with that crowd."

"Why does Emilian?"

"Wait." He holds up a finger. When he gets into the car he continues, "Emilian tends to entwine himself with the worst possible element we find in any town. Here, it's the werewolves."

"Not you, too." I roll my eyes. "What's so bad about them? Colin was nice to me."

"We have an unbeliever in the family." He chuckles. "Watch them. Observe them around town, but keep your distance."

"You're warning me, too?"

"Too?" Fonso's eyebrow rises.

"Kyle, from the diner, told me to be careful."

"I've seen him around." Fonso presses his lips together. "Watch Colin and his clan; see what you notice. Simply being observant can sometimes be a surprising gift."

"Yes, Yoda, all-seeing master." I laugh. "Maybe being observant is your special talent."

"Ha. Ha. And being attracted to trouble is yours."

"Touché."

Fonso changes the subject. "Did you really not know about us...Ma and Aunt Simza?" His brows furrow.

"Honestly, I didn't know you existed until yesterday. Why do you still live at home? You're twenty-four, right?"

"It's complicated." Fonso pauses. "I thought about leaving...several times actually, but Ma has a way of manipulating us. To her, it's important we stay together. The older we get, the harder it becomes for her. You heard Nadya yesterday talking about wanting to be like you and leaving. Ma says it's too dangerous to be separated...like we need to remain together to stay safe."

"Have you lived in many places?"

"For a long time...most of our lives, actually, we lived in a traveling carnival. We'd travel north in the summers and south in the winters. Aunt Simza was with us, too. Aunt Simza and Ma would read fortunes and talk to the dead. They were quite popular. There were other Roma with us. They ran several different booths and entertained in freak shows." His mouth sets in a hard line. "It all changed a few months ago.

"Aunt Simza said we had to leave. She was adamant. Ma freaked and they argued. We couldn't figure out what it was all about and Ma won't speak about it even now." Fonso turns the blinker on to turn into the campground. "We left and came here. Aunt Simza insisted on living on her own, but Ma visits her often. She's so stubborn. Whatever they fought about, or are fighting about, is bad. They've always been together and for this to break them apart—"

"Must have been extremely bad." I finish his sentence.

"But, Aunt Simza was right."

"About what?"

He pulls up to the cabin and looks at Aunt Simza's trailer. "After we left the carnival, one of my best friends, the snake charmer, called to tell me someone was hunting them. All the Roma left the carnival, a lot of them in body bags."

A shiver runs down my spine. It must be the Hunters.

He shakes his head. "Don't you have to be at work soon?"

"I, umm, I have a couple hours, but I'm starving. Do you want to get something to eat at the diner? I'll be happy to go in early."

"Sounds good to me." He smiles.

"Let me change. Come inside and give me a few minutes."

***

The diner isn't busy and Kyle isn't behind the grill.

Roger greets us when we sit. "Hey Alice! Are you here to eat before your shift?"

"I thought I'd try some of the food I've been serving. This is my cousin, Fonso."

"What can I get you?" Roger asks. I see he isn't holding a pad to write it down. "Sam is cooking now and he's the best."

"I won't tell Kyle you said that." I grin.

"Kyle knows it." He laughs. "I'm too outspoken not to say anything."

"I can see that."

"I'll have a burger, well done, with fries," Fonso says.

"With all the fixin's?" Roger asks.

He nods.

"I'll have the same." I give him our menus.

"Sounds good."

Roger tells Sam our order through the window instead of writing it down for him. No other server is here, and Abby is nowhere. It's a one-man show right before the night shift.

"I've never been here before." Fonso looks around the tiny diner.

"Do you have a job?" I ask.

"I work part-time at the bookstore, mainly on weekends. It gives me money for my car, but I end up spending more there than anywhere."

"What do you like to read?"

"Steampunk and Sci Fi mostly. I'll do the occasional fantasy, but often real life is crazier than what I read in a book."

"I can understand that."

"Do you like to read?"

Roger brings us water. "It'll be out in a moment." He goes back to the counter and wipes it down.

"I do, but I haven't in a while. I'm interested in the environment, marine biology, and some archeology, so I stick to the non-fiction section of the library." I tap my nails on the table. "I've taken several correspondence courses online because we never stay in one place long enough to go to college."

"We?"

Emptiness forms in my chest. "I meant my Dad and me, when we were together."

"Where is he now?"

I wish I knew. "I left him in Louisiana."

"And your Dad didn't tell you about us?"

The conversation takes a turn for the worse. I'm

not prepared to answer these questions, not knowing if I need to answer them truthfully.

"No."

"Here you go." Roger places our plates in front of us. "Bon appetite."

"Thank you," Fonso and I say in unison.

I immediately shove the burger in my mouth and take an enormous bite. "Mmm, amazing."

Roger smiles. "I know." He leaves us to enjoy the meal.

Fonso digs in too, and the questions stop. I'm relieved.

We finish our meals and Kyle walks through the front door. He waves.

Fonso stares at him. "That's Kyle, huh?"

"Yep. I guess that's my sign I need to start work." I dig into my bag. "Lunch is on me."

"No, I can't." Fonso reaches for his wallet.

"Nope, it's on me. Thank you for the ride and the rescue today." I glide over to the register and give Roger my money while stepping behind the counter.

Fonso follows me. "Thanks Alice."

"See you soon, I hope." I wave.

"You bet." He walks out and heads to his car.

"He seems like a nice fellow," Roger says, giving me my change.

"Keep it."

"No, Alice. I ain't no server and I'll take no tip

from ya."

Smiling, I take my money and shove it into my pocket. "Can I leave my bag somewhere safe?"

"Sure, in my office." He leads me through the kitchen where Kyle relieves Sam, the burly cook who makes a mean burger. "It's always unlocked, so you can squeeze in here and get it any time."

"Thanks." I set my bag in the office.

"Sure thing." He shuts the door and removes his apron. "I'll see you all later. It's you two tonight, so take it easy."

Sam and Roger leave out the back door together.

Kyle leans against the post at the kitchen entrance. "I'm sorry about this morning. I didn't mean to seem stalker-like."

"I didn't...I don't think you're stalking me." I clean the table Fonso and I sat at, bringing the dishes into the back.

"You didn't tell me yesterday that you knew Colin." I said. "You yelled at him for almost running me over, but you didn't mention you knew him from school."

"School?" Kyle's surprise gnaws at me. Did Colin lie?

"He said you went to school together." I wash my hands in the sink.

"We never went to school together. I'd be surprised if he even attended high school." Kyle goes back into the kitchen, grabbing pans and placing them on the stove.

"Why did he say that then?" I move to the window separating the kitchen from the counter.

The bell above the door rings and our first customer enters, taking me away from the conversation.

For the remainder of the evening, Kyle avoids me, cooking and doing kitchen tasks. When eleven o'clock rolls around, Roger comes in and closes the diner. Damn, I realize I missed the bus again. I need to ask Roger about leaving a few minutes early so I can catch it.

I wait for Kyle outside.

"Why were you avoiding me?" I cross my arms.

"I wasn't." He walks to his Jeep.

"Yes, you are." I walk behind him.

He breathes loudly. "I'm sorry. Colin is a sore subject."

"That's obvious."

"Do you want a ride home?"

Sheepishly, I lower my head. "Yes, thank you."

Once in the passenger seat, I repeat the question that's been lingering on my mind all night. "Why did Colin say you were in school together?"

"Colin and I trained together. It was in a fighting class, like martial arts."

We pass the bus stop. Colin stands by his truck

where he parked last night, watching me as Kyle drives past. Kyle doesn't see him. Colin's face heats with anger.

"It was a long time ago," Kyle continues. "I didn't like him then and I don't like him now."

"Thank you for telling me, and for the ride home."

"You're welcome."

We near the campground.

"You can drop me off here, at the entrance."

"Are you sure? I don't mind going in."

"Yes, I'm sure." I don't want to stir Deena or anyone else and draw attention.

"Okay, here you go." He pulls up to the entrance, turning his Jeep around.

"Thanks again."

He drives away, leaving me to think about Colin and the look he had when we passed. Guilt bubbles inside me. He was waiting for me and I ignored him.

On the way to my cabin, I see Fonso's car. Fonso stands outside Aunt Simza's trailer arguing with her.

CHAPTER 12

AUNT SIMZA SHAKES her head and slams the door in Fonso's face. He raises his arm and opens his hand. The ground shakes and a rock shoots through the air slamming into the closest tree trunk.

My mouth hangs open.

Fonso spots me and races in my direction. He slows when he nears me.

I raise my hand.

Fonso stops a few feet from me. "Alice, we need to talk."

"W-w-what was that?" I point to the tree trunk near Aunt Simza's trailer. "The rock just flew...without you touching it."

"I can explain." Fonso holds his hands up as if trying to hush me. "It's not what you think."

"Was I dreaming? I'm tired, for sure, but I'm certain of what I saw, damn it." I walk toward my cabin, ignoring him.

"Alice, please listen." He grabs my left arm.

I drop the cabin key.

He picks the key up and hands it to me.

"You told me you have no abilities. Your family said the same."

He lowers his head. "I lied."

I hold the door open for him. "Why?"

He exhales and walks inside. I gesture to the couch and he sits, making himself comfortable. "It's a long story."

I should have been exhausted from the day's events, but I was too pumped. "Let's hear it." I close the door and place my bag on the counter.

He scoots over, making room for me sit next to him. "First off, my family didn't lie to you. They don't know what I'm able to do."

"What was that?"

He leans on his side, facing me. "Telekinesis."

"What? Like moving things with your mind?" I ask. "What kind of things? How doesn't your family know this?"

"Aunt Simza knows. She's the one who told me to keep it a secret because it's a dangerous ability."

"Dangerous? How?"

"How much do you know about your mother?" He lifts an eyebrow.

"My mother?" A deep-seated sadness rises in the

pit of my stomach. "I don't know anything. Dad told me she died giving birth to me. She was beautiful, he told me, but I've never seen a picture, so I wouldn't know."

"He didn't mention her gift?"

"No."

"Aunt Simza told me she had the same ability I do. Her family knew and often used her for profit when she was younger. Our grandfather would charge fees for people to see her, like a circus freak. He used all of them, actually."

I was suddenly sick to my stomach and I was glad I hadn't eaten anything since the burger at lunch. I push the horrifying thought away and ask, "My mother was telekinetic?"

He nods. "Aunt Simza said she was very powerful. She could move boulders and buses. She could uproot trees and juggle hundreds of balls at the same time."

"And you, too?"

He shakes his head. "I'm not that strong. Aunt Simza said it's because I don't use it often. I'm suppressing it, because everything she's ever told me scared me. The only time something happens is when I'm angry."

I can relate. My emotions rule my ability. I open my mouth to say so, and then tighten my lips.

"How does your mother not know? Didn't you

always have this ability, even when you were young?" I remember all of those natural disasters that weren't so natural. They followed me to every town. Dad knew it from the moment I was born, or so he told me.

"I've always had it. Ma was so wrapped up in her drama...her problems...her ability, that she rarely paid attention to me. I've always been an introvert, so I spent a lot of the time by myself, playing alone."

"And Aunt Simza saw you?"

"Yes, she saw it when I was very young. She protected me, too. She'd coach me to not use my ability in front of anyone. She'd tell me the boogieman would come and snatch me. As I grew older, she told me other people would hunt me down if they knew what I could do. Just like..."

"Just like what?" My curiosity peaks and I feel my body stiffen.

"Like they hunted your mother."

I wasn't sure what I was expecting, but that wasn't it. "The Hunters," I whisper.

"What?" he asks.

By him confiding in me, it's like an instant bond has formed between us. When I glance up to meet his eyes, I feel I can trust him. "Dad told me she died giving birth to me." I'm filled with an overwhelming numbness.

"Aunt Simza said your mother and father ran

away from everyone before they had you. She figures the Hunters got her because Lyuba appeared to Aunt Simza."

It dawns on me that Aunt Simza speaks with the dead. "Did my mother tell her?"

"She didn't speak to Aunt Simza, she only appeared to let her know she'd passed. A warning to leave. That's when Aunt Simza, Ma, and Pa took me and ran. They escaped our grandfather and found refuge with a carnival. The first in a long line of changes."

"This is so much...I don't know what to think or say." My mind races. "Why were you arguing with her tonight? Aunt Simza, that is."

"She called Ma and told her she was leaving and this time she wanted to leave alone. She didn't want us to follow her or bother her anymore." He leans back and studies the ceiling. "She wouldn't tell me why. She's so angry. I have no idea why they are fighting and what is causing her to leave us. We've been together forever and it feels like she's abandoning us...me. She was the only one who knew."

"You trust her."

"She warned us if we were ever in danger. The dead always look out for her. Why would she put us in harm's way by leaving us?"

"I don't know."

105

"Will you keep my secret?" His eyes plead with me.

"Yes."

"Tell no one ever?"

"It's not my secret to share. I'd never do that to you."

"I believe you." He stands. "I'm going to go. I'm sure you're tired from working."

"Thank you, Fonso." I hug him. It's tempting to tell him my secret...the biggest secret of my life, but that warning written on a piece of paper enters my head. *Make sure no one learns of your ability...no one!*

He leaves and thoughts of my mother flood me. Did the Hunters get her? Did she really die like Dad had told me? I came here for answers, searching for my father, but all I find is more questions.

***

Low on clothes, I head into town early to shop. Filled with bags, I arrive at work and stuff them in Roger's office.

"Went shopping?" Kyle smiles. He flips a sizzling burger on the grill.

"Needed to get a few things. Running low on supplies."

"We aren't your storage unit, you know." Abby

pushes her retro looking glasses up her nose.

"Hush, Abby." Roger says. "You're getting crankier by the minute, I swear. Let's go home."

"You're married?" It came out of my mouth before I could hold it in and it sounded awful.

Roger laughs. "Going on forty-five years now, believe it or not."

"That may be all you're getting, you big oaf." Abby frowns.

"I'm sorry, that wasn't my place to ask."

"Don't worry your head none." Roger waves and rushes Abby out the door.

"It doesn't make sense, does it?" Kyle pokes his head through the window.

"Not at all." I put my apron on. "I don't know why I didn't pick up on it before."

"Because they don't act like a married couple." Kyle places two plates in the window. "Order."

The night flies by as a constant stream of diners come in. The tips feel heavy in my pocket and I don't feel so guilty for spending money on clothes today. All the extra money that was in that envelope is almost gone and I need to start buying groceries and paying rent soon.

Roger comes in at eleven and shoos us out, saying he'll help with the dishes since the washer guy didn't show tonight. Kyle took turns cleaning and cooking all night.

"I'll need you both back on Tuesday. Enjoy your days off."

"Thanks Roger."

Kyle holds the door open. "Seems like we are official work partners. I think Roger has ulterior motives."

"Huh?"

"We work together...the same hours, and now he's giving us the same time off?"

"Oh." My face feels flushed.

"Would you like to...if you're not too tired, that is...go watch the stars with me?" He rakes his hands through his hair.

"Now?" He shrugs. No one has ever asked me to go stargazing. "Okay. Sounds like fun."

"Really?" He grins. "Let's go. I have a great telescope. You will be amazed."

Kyle drives fifteen minutes west. "It's the best place to see the night clearly, away from the lights of the town and the coast."

He parks at the dead end of a dirt road.

"This is secluded."

He grabs his gear from the back, including a huge lens.

"Do you need help?" I ask.

"Can you take the bag? It has the tripod in it. That would help."

I follow him down a path to an open clearing.

LIGHTNING STRUCK

Grass and dandelions stand ankle high.

"Wow, you're right. It's so dark and the stars are so bright."

A few clouds pass over the hundreds of twinkling stars, making way for the clearest, liveliest night sky I've ever seen.

"Wait until you see it through the scope." Kyle sets it up and his enthusiasm entices me to be equally excited.

"You really are passionate about this."

"I've always been fascinated with space and the possibilities." He messes with the knob on the telescope as he looks through the lens. "Look at this."

I can see craters on the grayish moon. "That's amazing." I stare longer and see the cracks and wonder how big some of those holes are.

Pulling back, he readjusts the position.

"Here's another one that will blow you away. I'm so glad we can see it tonight." He backs away and lets me gaze.

"I can see the rings." It looks like two rings around Saturn. "It's so clear and seems so close."

He allows me to watch a while longer. I feel like I'm watching a *National Geographic* special. I pull back. "You want to see Jupiter?" he asks.

I nod.

He continues to show me a pinwheel galaxy, some clusters, and several planets in our solar system.

We move to the blanket when our space exploration finishes.

"I didn't know they could be so beautiful through the telescope like that. I mean, I've seen them on TV, but this is so pure and raw and real." My smile widens as we lay with our arms holding our heads up.

"I'm glad you enjoyed it." He turns on his side and faces me. "It's the best time to see it, on a clear night with no clouds. The weatherman says we are in store for showers tomorrow night, so I wanted to get out tonight and see what space had to offer me."

"Thank you for inviting me. I truly loved it."

"Alice?" I turn toward him, seeing his shadow silhouetted in the moonlight.

His hand finds the side of my neck. He leans in and my lips part. The kiss starts out slow and soft, but turns into long and passionate. I lean back, the side of his body pressing against me. He pulls back, smiling.

"I should get you home."

"Yes, that's probably a good idea." I could literally stay here all night and kiss him. There is something that feels different with him than Colin. Kyle is alluring in a more seductive way. His voice implies things his words doesn't and there are parts of me that tune into them and want them. Colin is thoughtful, yes, but our attraction to each other is raw, instinctual. He has a magnetic pull on part of my soul I can't resist.

LIGHTNING STRUCK

Kyle packs up and frees one of his hands to hold mine as we walk back to the Jeep.

"Thank you for coming with me tonight. I had a great time."

The ride home is quiet, but nice. He doesn't let go of my hand the entire time and it feels comforting. My thoughts travel to the way I ignored Colin, and a sour feeling settles in my gut.

He pulls up to my cabin. He leans across the console and kisses me lightly on my lips. "See you tomorrow?"

"Maybe."

He nods. "No reason to rush things." He waits for me to get inside before I hear his engine fade.

I lean against the inside of the door and bite my lower lip thinking about our kiss. When I step away, I notice a note on the floor.

It's not a love note...it's a warning.

Last Chance. Your dad's alive, but he won't be for long if you don't leave this place.

CHAPTER 13

I BANG ON Aunt Simza's door. "I know you're in there. Your dingy old truck is still here and you never go anywhere."

The trailer shakes as she walks through it. She opens the curtain, looking at me through the small window on the door. "Go away. I have nothing to say to you."

I shove the note against the window. "What's this then? Seems you have plenty to say, but not to my face."

Her eyes narrows. "I didn't write that, girl. Now go away."

"You didn't write this? So who did?" I lower the note. "Who knows about my dad? Why was your name given to me?"

Thunder rolls overhead; a downpour will start any minute.

Aunt Simza watches the dark sky. "You're

bringing nothing but trouble, just like I knew you would." She shuts the curtain and retreats to the back of the trailer.

The rain starts on the way to my cabin.

Doubt surfaces. If she didn't write that note, which she could be lying about, then someone here knows who I am and that I'm searching for dad.

Crashing into bed, I cry. Dad is in danger. He's out there, probably hurt and worrying about me. A sense of helplessness asphyxiates me; it feels like a boulder pushing against me and I'm powerless to free myself.

The storm drizzles and slows through the night, but I don't sleep. The sounds of the drops falling from the pine trees above soothes my mood. The tranquility of nature brings me solace in the darkness.

A knock at the door rouses me out of my waking slumber.

Fonso, red-eyed, stands with a large, black duffel bag. "Can I stay with you?"

"What's the matter?"

He plops the bag next to the couch.

"My telekinesis wasn't the only thing I was hiding." He sits.

"What?" I rub the sleepiness from my crusted eyes. "What happened?"

"I blew up at Ma and couldn't take it anymore. I let it slip. So much anger boiled inside of me that I popped." He flings his fingers in the air.

"You told her about the telekinesis?"

He turns crimson. "No. I told her I was gay."

I cover my mouth to hide the forming smile.

"You're going to laugh at me?" His mouth curves downward.

I shake my head. "She didn't know?"

"She refused to accept it, arguing about the importance of carrying on the line. She kept telling me 'No, you're not gay' as if it were a choice." He smacks his head. "I've never seen anyone more in denial in my life."

"What started all of this?"

"I confronted her about Aunt Simza and demanded to know what they were fighting about. It escalated from there."

"You didn't tell her about your gift though?"

"No, and I'm very proud about that, by the way. I wanted to blow her entire China collection out of the cabinet. It took great restraint to not do that." He leans back. "Did you know I was gay?"

"It's not a big deal. I don't dwell on stuff, but I figured you were."

"Ma is so antiquated. She's living in a different century, still wearing long skirts, short tops, headscarves, and massive jewelry." He looks as me. "Doesn't she realize her kids are born in modern times? Things change and she can't seem to understand that. I told her I was leaving. I couldn't live with her and her old ways anymore."

"Did she freak?"

"She kept mumbling about her keeping us safe and we would die without her."

"Why did she do that?"

"Because she's delusional. All she can do is read past lives. Aunt Simza was the one keeping us safe, and now she's leaving."

"Speaking of Aunt Simza." I show the note to Fonso.

Last Chance. Your dad's alive, but he won't be for long if you don't leave this place.

"What's this?"

"I came home last night and found that stuffed under my door."

"Your dad?"

Time to reveal the truth. "I came down here to find him. I didn't leave him. I think he's been taken by the Hunters. That note with Aunt Simza's name was my only clue to finding any information about him. I think Aunt Simza knows about Dad and she wants me to leave for fear the Hunters will find her."

"I don't think this is Aunt Simza's writing. Plus, she said she's leaving, so I don't think she would try to warn you away." His eyebrows furrow. "Did you ask her about it?"

"I banged on her door last night, but she said she

didn't write it. She said I'm bringing trouble, though, so she knows something."

"Someone knows why your here, though." He places the note on the coffee table. "Why didn't you tell us all this before?"

"I didn't, and still don't know whom to trust. I don't know who sent me the note about Aunt Simza, but it also said don't..."

"Don't what?"

"It also said to keep secrets and not tell anyone anything." I lie. It's becoming too easy to talk with Fonso.

"Is your real name Alice?"

I shake my head. Embarrassed to admit I've lied, but he's been so open with me, and...I need to start telling the truth some time. "No. It's Elysia."

"That makes more sense. You look like an Elysia. Definitely not an Alice." He laughs.

"I like Alice." I shove him. "We are so used to using different names everywhere we go."

"You've moved around a lot, too, huh?" He lifts his legs up onto the coffee table. "How did you get away?"

"Dad came to my apartment in the morning and told me it was time to leave. He had a bag packed for me and he didn't give me time to grab anything else. He was adamant I leave, but he wasn't coming with me."

"He has a gift?"

"He knows when trouble is coming." I slap the pillow on the couch in frustration. "Why he didn't come with me, I'll never understand. We always moved together. He protected me." I feel myself getting hysterical and I need to calm my nerves before I bring on a tidal wave.

Fonso rests his hand over mine. The surging of anger in my veins slows. "Maybe he thought you'd be safer without him."

"He told me he needed to take care of a few things, but he never showed up at the place we were supposed to meet. Two Hunters did, though."

His eyes widen, as if I told him I saw a ghost, and fear found its way across his soft features. "You saw them? What happened?"

"A woman and a man had tracked me down. I got a strange phone call warning me they were there. When I saw them, I started running. I didn't see the man too well, but I was face to face with the woman. It won't be any time too soon that I'll forget her. She got a good look at my right hook though."

"My cousin, the bad ass." He smiles.

"So, I came here. A cryptic note leads me to Cassadaga and I run into a family I never knew about. Yeah, strange things seem to follow wherever I go."

A knock at the door causes both of us to jump.

"I got it." Fonso rises, answering the door.

"Wow."

A huge bouquet of flowers hides the delivery person's face.

"Thanks." Fonso takes them and closes the door. "Doesn't seem like all bad things are happening to you." He places them on the counter, grabbing the note attached to the top. "To Alice—"

I snatch it from him. "That's the biggest arrangement I've ever seen." White, pink and yellow lilies mix in with pink roses and white carnations.

"Who's it from?" Fonso leans in to smell a rose. "These aren't the cheap ones, either. You can smell a strong rose scent."

Alice, I had a wonderful time with you last night. Please have dinner with me tomorrow night.

"It's from Kyle." I look at Fonso. "And, he left me his number."

"The dreamy guy you work with?" He grabs the note from me. "What did you two do last night?" He nudges my arm.

"He took me stargazing."

"Stargazing? Are you kidding me?" Fonso places the invitation on the counter. "He sends you flowers to ask you out on another date. Brilliant execution."

I shove him.

"Look who's blushing." He points at my face.

"I'm not blushing."

"Did you do anything other than gaze at the stars

last night?" He wiggles his eyebrows.

"Maybe." I bite my lip and smile.

"You floozy."

"We kissed. That's it." I walk around to the kitchen and pour a glass of orange juice. "It's probably a bad idea to date someone I work with, isn't it? I shouldn't be doing this."

"Yes, you should." He displays the flowers as if pretending to be Vanna White.

"Fine. I'll go." I roll my eyes.

"That took a lot of convincing." He smiles. "I wonder where he'll take you. Maybe he'll take you out of town. There're not many good choices nearby."

"I'll call him later."

"You better." He presses his hands together as if praying. "So, Elysia, dear cousin, can I crash with you?"

"There's only one bed, but I'll talk with Deena. Maybe she'll make you a deal with one of the other cabins. Until then, you're welcome to the couch."

"Thanks."

"First, you have to help me with something."

"What's that?" He places the juice back into the empty fridge. "Oh."

"Yeah, can you take me grocery shopping?"

"Sure thing. Let's do this." He holds his glass up and clinks it with mine. "Too bad these aren't mimosas."

I take a sip. "We can rectify that situation."

We laugh.

***

Heading into town, we stop at the diner to retrieve my bags I accidently left. We decide to travel further to hit a discount store to buy cheaper groceries and a few cleaning supplies. I also get a new pair of sandals to replace the ones I left at the beach when I was with Colin.

Fonso visits the liquor store and refuses to tell me what he bought.

"Why are you being so secretive?"

"Why are you being so nosy?" he quips.

When we return home, I feel like cleaning so I sweep the cabin.

Fonso puts the groceries away.

"Here you go." He brings me a light orange drink in a clean glass, holding his own in his other hand. "Now, we have mimosas."

I take a sip. "That's good."

"Another of my many talents: bartender extraordinaire."

"Yes, you're a master with orange juice and champagne." I laugh. "It's really good though."

"It's the type of champagne you use. Nothing but

the best."

"Cleaning with mimosas. That's a first for me." I start in on the bathroom, scrubbing the toilet and cleaning the shower.

Fonso makes the bed and puts my clothes away on the new hangers we bought.

It begins to feel like I have a roommate and friend again. I keep reminding myself he's family and I don't need to pretend around him. He knows I'm Elysia. There's only one thing I didn't tell him...one thing I promised Dad I'd never tell anyone.

"Did you call Kyle?" Fonso yells through the bedroom.

"Not yet."

"It's getting late."

The sun sinks on the horizon. The day has gotten away from us as we drank and cleaned. "I didn't realize it was so late." I come into the living room and see the flowers on the counter. "I'll call him after I take out the trash."

Fonso grabs the trash bag out of the kitchen. "I can take it out."

"No, let me, please. Maybe I'll run into Deena and talk with her."

He hands me the trash. "Okay, but call him as soon as you get back." He places his smartphone on the counter.

"Deal."

The one street light switches on over the campground office. Deena's dark trailer, coupled with her missing car tells me she's not here. I'll have to make it a point to go over early to see her.

The sun exits as I near the putrid green trash bin. Surveying the grounds, I see no lights...no fires...no early partiers. It's quiet and still. Aunt Simza's trailer light remains on. Maybe she'll speak with Fonso tomorrow. I know he'll try again. At least she hasn't left, yet.

A rustling in the woods grabs my attention. Expecting a raccoon to peek out, I'm surprised when a russet wolf appears. It steps in my path, blocking my way home. It bares its teeth and growls.

CHAPTER 14

MY HEART RACES when the wolf lowers its body, positioning itself to strike. This isn't good.

"Whoa, you stay there, dog."

It snaps, snarling at me.

I slowly walk back toward the trash bin...the closest cover.

It matches my steps, toying with me. If it were hungry, it would have struck by now. It lunges. I run behind the trash bin and circle around, leaving the wolf on the opposite side. There's no way I can outrun it, but I have to try. I race toward the cabin. The wolf follows and a tug at my ankle takes me down. Its teeth have a good chunk of pants in its mouth, along with a bit of my skin. My instincts kick in and I stomp its head with my free leg, causing it to loosen its clenching jaws.

Hail falls fast, pummeling us with bigger than

normal round ice balls.

The wolf shakes its head and gets back on its feet at the same time I do.

The cabin is less than 15 feet away, but by the look in the wolf's eyes, it will attack before I can make it.

A hailstone the size of a baseball smacks onto its back and a squeal escapes its jaw. It recovers and jumps toward me. I raise my arms, knowing it'll chomp into them within seconds.

Out of the corner of my eye, a shadow flashes by. I lower my arms to see another wolf in midair blocking my attacker. They tumble in the dirt snapping at each other.

The brown one convulses on the ground. It yelps and hollers, while changing into flesh and blood. It's Kayla.

The other one rises, shakes, and turns into Colin.

"Get out of here, now!" he yells at Kayla.

She scowls at me and runs off into the woods, stark naked.

Colin faces me, also naked and sweating. The hail falls in smaller pebbles, turning into heavy raindrops the closer he walks to me. He stops a few feet away.

Emilian was right. They are werewolves.

"Elysia!" Fonso steps onto the porch. He sees Colin and his gaze trails down his body. "Are you okay?"

"Elysia?" Colin asks.

"I'm fine." I glance toward Fonso and mouth the words again. He looks at me and then at Colin before retreating inside.

"You're name isn't Alice. You lied." Colin crosses his arms.

"And, you're a fucking werewolf, so I'd say we're even." I take off my shirt, leaving me in my bra, and toss it to him. "Cover up."

He holds it over his groin. "I never pretended to be otherwise. We don't go around announcing our heritage."

"Your girlfriend tried to kill me." The shock of seeing him in wolf form hits me and I sit on the porch step. "You're a werewolf and your girlfriend tried to eat me."

"Kayla isn't my girlfriend." He steps closer and kneels in front of me with my shirt strategically placed. "Not anymore. It was over a long time ago, but she can't let go."

"So she goes around eating potential threats?" I rub my temples. "You're a werewolf."

He grabs my hands. The electric mini-shock pulses through me and releases a calming feeling.

"She's jealous. She knows I'm into you and it upsets her. I'm sorry she came out here and tried to hurt you. I won't allow it to happen again." He smiles.

"What are you smiling about?"

"You called yourself a potential threat, so does that mean I have a chance?" He leans closer and brushes the hair from my face, sending a flurry of excitement through me.

"I...um...you're a..." I stumble with my thoughts and the right words. Kyle pops into my head. His sweetness and patience with me when we were stargazing tug at my chest. The flowers...those beautiful eyes.

"I'm a werewolf. There are no more secrets between us, Elysia." Colin's dark chestnut eyes penetrate me. My name on his lips awakens a burning desire; a feeling so alien it's spine-chilling, yet utterly arousing. "Are there any more secrets?" He doesn't give me a chance to answer before he leans in. Our lips are only millimeters apart. My breath quickens. The air around us stirs and a breeze lifts strands of my hair. "The name Elysia is almost as beautiful as you." He pulls me up, wraps his hand around my neck, and kisses me. My shirt falls to the ground and I feel him against me...his eagerness, unable to hide.

It feels as if a hundred sparklers light inside me all at once. My body quivers as the kiss deepens. He peels slowly away. My eyes remain closed as he places his forehead against mine.

"I'll take that...for now." He backs away and runs toward the trees.

LIGHTNING STRUCK

My knees weaken. I sit back on the porch, pulling my shirt over me. A howl erupts in the woods.

"Elysia?" Fonso peeks out of the cabin.

"Huh?" My fuddled, foggy mind clears. "I'm coming."

"What happened?" He holds the door open for me. "Your jeans are all ripped."

"I was attacked by a werewolf. That jealous bitch from the beach. She's a fucking werewolf." My lower lip trembles. "Colin's a fucking werewolf."

"And you thought we were lying?" Fonso closes the door. "They've been tormenting our kind for millennia, and you thought they were make-believe monsters?"

"But, Emilian..."

"Emilian thinks these wolves are different. He says they aren't like the others. They can be trusted, but he's wrong."

"Werewolves exist," I say in a daze and plop on the couch.

"We've covered this, I thought."

"He kissed me." I touch my lips.

"Colin? The naked werewolf kissed you?" Fonso sits next to me. "You let him?"

"I...um...he caught me by surprise."

"I can't believe it. You're here two fucking days and already you have two gorgeous men pinning over you and I've been here months and nothing." He chuckles. "Maybe you are trouble."

I playfully shove him. "What am I going to do?"

"You're going to call Kyle and accept his date. Right now." Fonso gets his phone from the counter and presses it into my hand. "Those flowers weren't cheap, girl."

"But, Colin..."

"But Colin nothing. Did Colin send you expensive-ass flowers? No!" He pushes my hand with the phone in it. "Kyle's number is punched in. Hit send."

"You're like a drug dealer." I poke him.

"You're the floozy."

"That's not funny." I pout. After hitting the button, I take the phone into my room.

"Hello?" Kyle answers.

"Hi Kyle. It's Alice." I pause. My stomach feels like the mimosas are swishing around inside.

"Hey." He sounds eager. "How's it going?"

"I received your invitation. Thank you for the flowers. They are beautiful."

"You're welcome. So, are we on for tomorrow?"

"Yes."

"Great. Pick you up at 6?" He asks.

"See you then."

"Have a good night."

"You, too." I hang up and fall back onto the bed.

I stare at the fan circling, imagining it's the top of

a helicopter. Maybe it'll take me far away to a deserted island free of problems. Colin pops into my mind. I touch my lips and wonder if I'll ever feel a kiss like that again.

***

The morning dew blankets the pine needles, making them look like mini icicles. I pull my hair up into a ponytail and begin to jog in the forest. Keeping in line with the rising sun, I keep an even pace. Once I hit the road, I follow it north, away from town. Coming close to Cassadaga, I see a morning yoga class, and turn back toward the campground.

It feels peaceful listening to the sounds of the forest. Most runners prefer music, but it's nature that soothes me. I ran longer than I expected, so the last mile I walk back. When I enter the campground, I see Deena head toward the office.

"Hey." I catch my breath. "Can I talk to you?"

"Hi Alice. You've been busy this morning already, I see. I'm exhausted looking at you." She holds her hand over her eyes, blocking the sun's rays.

"It feels good to jog every once in a while." I hold the door open for her. "My cousin popped in last night, needing a place to crash for a while, and—"

"He needs one of the cabins soon." Deena nods. "I figured as much when I saw his car parked by your cabin. He usually visits Madame Aishe."

"Yes. I swear sometimes you can read my mind."

She touches some keys hanging behind the counter and plucks one down. "Here's an extra key to your cabin, but same rules apply."

"Got it." I hug her. "You're the best."

"Oh, I know." She grins. "Get out of here."

I race to my cabin and open the door to a delicious scent of fried buttery bread.

"Deena said you can stay with me, but if the owner ever comes to town we'll have to leave." I watch Fonso fix grilled cheeses on the stove. "I'm sure she'll give you the same deal on your own cabin, too, when you need it."

"That's great." He turns them over. "I'll have to find a full-time job now and we can save up money to have a stash when needed."

The way he says 'we' makes me feel a part of a family again. It's so easy with him. He's the big brother I never knew I wanted. "She's cool."

"I talked to Aunt Simza this morning. Well, she talked through the window. She won't even open the door for me now." He scoops the sandwiches onto two plates, placing one in front of me.

"Thanks."

"I told her I was staying with you."

"What'd she say?"

"She said I was a damn fool and I should go back

to my mother." He chomps into his sandwich.

"She doesn't like me. What does she think I'll do? Corrupt you?"

"She says you attract trouble and more trouble is bound to come to me if I stay. Then I told her that trouble has always followed us everywhere, so why is now so different?"

"And?"

"She didn't say one more word. She closed her curtain and walked away from me."

"This is good." I hold my grilled cheese up. "Extremely buttery."

"I like to eat." He pats on his bulging stomach. "What are you wearing on your date tonight?"

"I figure I'd go completely nude and stir things up." His eyes bulge and I roll my eyes. "Jeans and a top. What I always wear."

"That's classy." He bangs his glass down too hard, causing milk to slosh out the side. "What if he takes you to a fancy restaurant and you feel underdressed?"

"Now you're making me anxious."

"I'm sure Colin wouldn't mind you showing up naked. Werewolves are very free with their bodies."

"You don't like him much, do you?"

"No. I don't like what I've seen of him. He's not a good person."

"You warned me about him before. When you

picked me up at the beach. Is there something you're not telling me?"

"I think they bully some of the townspeople."

"What do you mean, bully?"

"He's a damn werewolf. They are known for bullying. Do you ever see any of them work? No. When we traveled with the carnival, we ran into quite a lot of them. They weren't nice. They've been chasing our kind for a long time. I don't care what Emilian says. I don't trust them."

"What do you mean chasing?"

"We'll talk later. Get ready for your date. I don't want to give another history lesson now." He blows a kiss at me. "I have to go find another job."

"Here." I dig in my pocket. "Deena gave me an extra key for you."

"Love Deena." He walks out the door, locking it behind him.

Viewing my wardrobe, I fear Fonso's right. I don't have anything fancy. If Kyle shows up in a nice suit, I'm screwed.

Dusk descends. I hear Kyle's Jeep and peek through the curtain. Kyle parks in front of my cabin and gets out. He's wearing a long-sleeved flannel and jeans...thank goodness.

I open the door before he climbs the stairs. "Hi."

"Hi." He leans in and kisses me. It's a quick, sweet kiss, but reminds me of the longer one we had under the stars two nights ago. "You look nice."

"Thank you. So do you." I grab my bag and lock the door. "Where are we going?"

"Do you like Italian?"

"Yum."

"Then I know the perfect place."

He holds my hand for the duration of the 20-minute ride south. The restaurant sits on a lakeside, with candlelit tables outside. "This is pretty."

The hostess seats us at a secluded table near the water.

"What's your favorite Italian food?" Kyle asks as he reads the menu.

"Chicken Parmigiana." I lick my lips. "Yours?"

"Veal Parmigiana."

"Baby cows? That's awful."

"Don't judge me." He smiles.

We place our orders. A soft breeze blows in. Frogs croak near the lake edge. "It's beautiful out tonight."

The waitress returns with our drinks. "It is. It's even nicer that you're here with me." He passes the sweeteners over. I refuse. "No sugar in your tea? How could you make such a mistake?"

"I thought this was a judgment-free zone?" I smirk.

"Ok. Ok. Judge-free zone. Can we now get all the bad first date questions out of the way?"

"Bad first date questions? I can't wait to hear them."

"You know...the questions you're not supposed to ask people that tend to scare them away. I'm apparently great at that."

"There's your flaw. I knew it was bound to pop up soon. What's the first question?"

"Where were you born?" He leans on the table, putting on a serious face.

"Yes, that's an awful first date question. I'm ready to walk out."

We laugh.

"I was born in California. You?"

"Florida. Both coast state babies. That's why we're drawn to each other." His shoulders relax. "Here's a tough one. It's a fill-in-the-blank. Last relationship failed because...?"

"He asked too many stupid questions."

"This is why I'm single, ladies and gentlemen." He waves his hands in the air to an empty audience.

Our food arrives and we start eating. It's delicious...probably one of the top three dinners I've ever eaten of all time.

"Is it my turn?" I ask when the server takes the plates away. "To ask questions, that is."

"Shoot."

"Do you live alone?"

"Yes. Staying in an apartment a few blocks from

the diner."

"And you don't walk to work?"

"If I walked to work, how could I drive you home?" His mouth twists into a lopsided smile.

"Ah, it's your power tool of seduction."

"I've never heard that analogy before, but I like it."

"Do you have family near here? Are they also in Florida? Any siblings?"

His smile disappears. "My mother died seven years ago. My dad lives on the coast, but we don't talk much. I'm an only child. What about you?"

An ache builds within me. We have more in common than he realizes. I'm not sure I can muster a response.

A steady rain starts, blowing the wetness in with the breeze.

Kyle moves to cover me from getting wet. "Here are my keys to the Jeep. I'll go inside to pay the bill and meet you." He looks up to the sky with a baffled expression. "I thought it wasn't supposed to rain tonight."

I nod and rush to his Jeep. Once I'm inside, I look for a towel or something to dry my face, but his back seat is bare. I open the glove box and a gun tumbles out into my hand.

CHAPTER 15

THE GUN FEELS heavy in my hand. A shiver runs through me when I shakily place it back into the glove compartment. Why does a diner cook/stargazer feel the need to carry a gun?

I've never liked guns.

Kyle runs to the Jeep. "Phew, it's coming down now."

"Yeah, do you have a towel, napkin, or tissue? My face is wet." I slowly reach for the glove box.

He grabs my hand. "Not in there. I have a blanket in the back."

He doesn't want me to see the gun. "That's okay. Don't worry about it. Wouldn't want you to get any wetter."

"Did you want to see a movie or something? No stargazing tonight, unfortunately." He starts the engine. "It's early enough to catch the last showing in town."

LIGHTNING STRUCK

"Kyle, I'm actually not feeling too well. My head's pounding. I'm afraid I'll have to take a raincheck, if that's okay."

He squeezes my hand. "Do you need me to pick you up anything on the way home? Aspirin?"

"No, that's not necessary. I have something at home." I close my eyes, leaning against the headrest. "Thank you, though. Thanks for dinner and for the flowers, too. They are gorgeous."

"You're welcome."

Kyle remains quiet during the ride home. He turns on the radio, playing soft classical music with the volume low. All I can think about is the gun one foot in front of me. The gun he didn't want me to see.

Why did I need to test him? I honestly thought he'd justify its existence, easing my mind from coming up with wild and crazy accusations. Maybe he's a hitman and the diner is his cover. Maybe he's been threatened. Maybe he's a loon. Why didn't he let me open the damned glove box?

"We're here." Kyle pats my shoulder.

I rub my eyes open. "Oh."

"Is someone staying with you?" He points to Fonso's car.

"That's my cousin's. He's crashing here for a while. Feeling kind of crowded at home." I pick up my bag. "Thank you for dinner. It was a great choice."

"You're welcome." He leans in, pecking me on the lips.

"See you tomorrow at the diner?"

He nods.

I hop out of the Jeep, dashing in the drizzle to the cabin.

He drives away before I'm through the door and I'm relieved.

"How'd the date with Mr. Dreamy go?" Fonso lowers his paperback. "Where'd he take you?"

"We went to an Italian restaurant by a lake. It was good." I fling my bag onto the coffee table.

"Good? Just good? Not fabulous or amazing or even a wonderful?" He places his book on the floor. "Why are you home so early?"

"It started raining and I told him I had a headache."

"A headache? Why? What happened?"

I face him. "It started raining and I went to his Jeep while he was paying. I looked in his glove box for a napkin or something and an effing gun falls in my hand."

"A lot of people have guns these days." Fonso shrugs.

"That's not the weird part. I put the gun back and when he came out I reached for the glove compartment, pretending to look for a tissue and he grabbed my hand away. He didn't want me to see it.

Why be so secretive?"

"You tested him." He ticks his tongue against the roof of his mouth. "Why do women analyze everything all of the time?"

"Come on. Tell me that's not suspicious. All he had to do was tell me it was in there and why. How hard is that?"

"Instead of asking him, you faked a headache to end the date?"

"It felt off...like it wasn't right."

"Could this be because of a certain naked werewolf from last night?" He purses his lips. "He gave you flowers. He took you to see the stars. He drives a Jeep."

"What does a Jeep have to do with anything?"

"Jeeps are sexy." He scrunches his eyebrows together.

I laugh.

"What? They are." He picks his book back up. "You're in my bed, by the way."

"That's the first time a guy's ever said that to me in such a negative way." I get up, smiling.

"Well, with your manners, it probably won't be the last." He flips a page.

"Good night, Fonso." I bend and peck him on the cheek.

"Good night, Floozy." He winks.

***

"Wake up! Wake up!" Fonso bounces on my bed.

"What are you doing?" I throw a pillow at him.

"We need to go to the mall."

"Why? With what money?" I sit up. "I hate shopping unless absolutely necessary."

"I have an interview and I don't want to go alone. They called last night and with the whole gun thing, I forgot to tell you."

"Oh, well then I'll go. Give me a few minutes."

"That's all you have." He leaves, shutting my door behind me.

I had slept later than I planned. Forgoing the shower, I throw my hair up in a ponytail and hurry out to see Fonso chomping on cereal. He shoves the last bite into his mouth and sets the bowl into the sink. "Good, let's go."

"Are you late?"

"Maybe a little."

"For an interview? You're insane." I laugh, grabbing my bag. "Where's the mall?"

"Twenty to thirty minutes away, close to the coast."

We pile into the car. "What are you interviewing for?"

"Some small gimmicky store. You know, the ones that sell all the gag gifts."

"I don't go to many malls. I try to avoid them at all costs."

"You have no sense of style, do you?" His smile fades. "Who will I shop with if I can't convince you to go with me?"

"First of all, you should be saving your money. Second, who did you shop with before?"

"Nadya was my partner in that department. I bet she's upset I left. She has no ride now, other than Emilian and he's too selfish most of the time to take her any where."

"Does she know?"

"Know what? That I'm gay?" He nods. "She's the only one who understood. Emilian didn't even know. He's too wrapped up in his make-believe world to pay attention to anything or anyone else."

"Make believe?"

"Isn't that what you thought about the werewolves? They are fantasy, right?"

"They called him their mascot." I recall Colin's words. *Colin—* My thoughts go in a direction I'm not sure I want them to. I cut them off before I start thinking too hard or deep about him or my feelings.

"That doesn't surprise me. He never knew how to make real friends. Then again, Ma never really wanted us too."

We pass through town. Colin's truck is parked in the corner lot.

"Speaking of the Devil." Fonso spots it, too.

He slows down as we pass the barber shop. Colin

stands outside with Riley, Brayden, Kayla, and an older man. "What are they doing?"

"Remember when I told you to watch them?"

Colin sees me, and his jaw tightens. He turns away, pretending to look in a real estate office window.

"Yeah?" I say.

"They take money from people, Elysia. I told you they weren't good."

"That's not right. It can't be. He wouldn't—"

"You're seeing it now. That old guy owns the barber shop."

I watch the three of them leave the shop counting money in the rearview mirror. "Why?"

"Extortion. They do it to Jared at the bookstore, too. They claim they are protecting the town and all the people in it. Everyone needs to pay them a fee."

"How is this happening in this day and age? This is something from the mobster era. Why doesn't he report it?" *Colin... stealing.* He doesn't seem like he could do something like that. No one around here is what they seem.

"This town doesn't have its own police department or sheriffs. They rely on the neighboring town's sheriff department, who's more concerned with drug busts and patrolling the coast than a small hick town near the psychic capital of the world."

"I'm in shock."

LIGHTNING STRUCK

Fonso remains silent throughout the remainder of the ride to the mall.

I wait by a fountain while he goes into the store for his interview. A tidal wave of disappointment overcomes me when I think about Colin and how he avoided eye contract while his pack extorted money from an innocent man. It made me think about Roger and if he's one of the victims. Should I ask or would that bruise his ego? Would Kyle know about it? The way Kyle yelled at him for almost running me over...he probably has no clue.

"All done." Fonso sits next to me.

"And?"

"I got the job. They will work around my bookstore hours on the weekend, so I can keep that, too." A prideful smile lights up his face.

"Congrats!" I hug him. "How could anyone not want to hire a catch like you?"

I see Nadya and Emilian coming toward us.

"Told you I'd find them," Nadya says.

"Oh, great." Fonso sighs. "What are you guys doing here?"

"Ma sent us to find you." Kayla holds her hand out and Emilian puts five dollars in it. "Emilian didn't think you'd be here."

"Dude, why do you ever bet against her?" Fonso stands, backhanding his shoulder in jest.

"I don't know." Emilian says. "I didn't think

you'd be at the damn mall."

"We go to the mall all the time, doofus." Nadya rolls her eyes.

"You found us. What does Ma want now? I'm not moving home again." Fonso twists his head, beckoning me to leave with him.

"She wants to invite you and Alice to dinner. She wants to make things right." Nadya explains. "How can you leave her like that?"

"This from the girl who wants to be on her own?" Fonso gives her a half-smile. "Oh, I want to be like you, Cousin Alice. I want to be on my own." He mimics Nadya's voice well.

Nadya sticks her tongue out at Fonso. "That's not me at all."

"Are you coming or not?" Emilian asks. "I have places to be."

"Like with your wolf buddies, robbing the townspeople of their hard earnings?" I ask, the words coming out in a flurry of madness before I can stop them.

"What? No. They don't..." Emilian begins.

Nadya and Fonso stop and leer at him.

"It's not what you think." Emilian says. "They have to."

"Right." I say. "You tell Colin that I don't want to see him again, and to keep that crazy bitch away from me."

LIGHTNING STRUCK

"Let's go." Fonso says.

"Are you coming to Ma's?" Nadya asks.

Fonso looks at me and I shrug. This is up to him.

"Fine. We'll come for a few minutes and that's all. She has to get to work later." Fonso says.

"Can I ride with you, then?" Nadya asks. " Emilian's truck stinks."

"Does not!" Emilian yells. "Whatever." He storms out of the mall in a different direction.

I feel guilty. Emilian didn't deserve to be snapped at over the company he keeps. I shouldn't have been so nasty, but I was angry over Colin's criminal and immoral actions.

We drive to Aunt Mirela's house, Nadya filling us in on all that's been happening. Aunt Mirela's been a wreck over Aunt Simza and Fonso; her clients aren't coming in for as many readings; Nadya's been stuck at the house with no one to talk to. Her incessant blabbering made me want to stick my head out the window. As much as I enjoy having a female cousin, she really needs to get a job, and some friends. She's a lot like her mother, but she would hate me if I ever told her that.

"We're here." Fonso announces to stop Nadya's complaining.

I follow Nadya inside.

"What's happening?" Nadya asks.

Aunt Mirela stands next to Emilian, somberness

145

plastered on their faces.

She holds out her hand revealing a black stone.

Emilian does the same. "It was in my truck."

Fonso walks in, the same worried look on him. "This fell out of my visor." He holds up another black stone.

"What do they mean?" I ask.

"It means our time has run out." Aunt Simza stands in the doorway, holding the same stone up. "They're coming for us."

CHAPTER 16

AN EERIE SILENCE falls over the room. It's the first time I've been around my newfound family when they have nothing to say.

Aunt Simza enters the home and sits on the couch. It's the closet I've been to her. She doesn't look at me. She stares blankly at the corner of the room, where a plant sits on a stand.

Nadya pulls out a table chair and plops into it, a tear forming in her eye.

Fonso and Emilian stand side-by-side, arms crossed, as if they were two statues guarding the room.

Aunt Mirela sits next to Aunt Simza. She pats her hand.

"This is her fault," Aunt Simza breaks the silence. "She brought this to us."

"She's Lyuba's daughter," Aunt Mirela says. "She's family. You know this."

"Doesn't matter," Aunt Simza replies. "She's brought bad luck."

"I'm standing right here." I wave. "Can someone tell me what or who is coming for us? The significance of the black stones?"

"It means we have to leave," Aunt Mirela explains. "That's all it means. We have to leave. Together and tomorrow."

"We've never gotten black stones before." Fonso throws his stone onto the coffee table. "It's a warning from them."

"Them who?" I ask.

"We're not sure who they are." Aunt Mirela sighs. "It's an old superstition, nothing more. We just need to move and stick together."

"You've told us tales when we were younger, Ma. This wasn't a joke then. You said if the stones showed up, the family disappeared. Vanished. Never to be heard from again." Fonso paces in the tiny living room. "Now you say it's a silly superstition."

"I should have left the moment I saw you." Aunt Simza glares at me. "We would have been safe here another ten months or so had you not shown up."

"What is your problem with me?" I ask. "I came here looking for you because I was given a note with your name on it. Some loving family I find. You shut the door in my damned face when I needed someone most." I point my finger at her. Heat rises within me and thunder booms in the distance.

"We are not the enemy." Aunt Mirela shakes her head. "We need to stop fighting with one another and work together to solve this. We pack up and leave in the morning. That's what we have to do." Aunt Mirela stands. She looks around the trailer. "We can't take it all. Pack only the necessities and we take what we can fit in Aunt Simza's trailer, Fonso's car, and Emilian's truck. No furniture. Just the basics."

"I ain't going with you." Aunt Simza stands and heads toward the door. "I can't."

"Simza!" Aunt Mirela grabs her shoulders, turning her around to face her. "We are family. We stick together. We need each other to survive."

Aunt Simza lowers her head. "I know, damn it. I know."

Aunt Mirela's mouth forms a tight smile. "We will get through this. Join another carnival?"

"Is she coming?" Aunt Simza nods in my direction.

"Yes, she's coming. We are all leaving together." Aunt Mirela looks around the room at each one of us. "Pack all you can, meet here in the morning at six. We head north."

An aching uneasiness forms in the pit of my stomach.

Aunt Simza nods and leaves.

"See, we will be fine. Aunt Simza is coming with

us. We will get through this." Aunt Mirela brushes her skirt, smoothing out the few wrinkles. "I need to make some calls." She looks at me. "Cancel appointments and such. Fonso, help your cousin pack. You both are welcomed to come back tonight and stay here, if you want."

"We'll be fine. See you in the morning." Fonso motions me to follow.

"Bye." I glance at Emilian. He continues to stare at the floor, a distance building in his eyes.

"Are you okay?" Fonso asks, as we get into the car.

"I'm still processing."

"This is not how I expected my day to go. To think I just got a fucking job." Fonso bangs on the steering wheel a few times. "I hate moving. I hate starting over. I'm getting sick of this."

"Did those stones really scare you?"

"When I was younger, Ma told me the stones were a bad omen. It meant death was coming and the only way to escape death was to move. If you didn't keep moving, it would catch up to you and take you. Then she'd tell me scary stories about people disappearing and all that other nonsense."

"You didn't believe her?"

"It's not that. It's that she was always so serious when she told her stories. She believed them."

"Are you happy Aunt Simza is going?"

"I hope she does. Hopefully, whatever feud they had, this will end it. Maybe this is a blessing in disguise...a change that will bring us all back together again." His lips curve downward.

"Is that what you want?"

"I don't know."

"I forgot I have to work tonight." I stare out the window.

"Why bother? You'll just be leaving tomorrow."

"Might as well go. It's not like I have much to pack, plus we can always use the money." I'm filled with an overwhelming dread. I was sent to this place to find Aunt Simza, but I'm still nowhere closer to discovering the whereabouts of Dad. Now, I'm running again from another potential threat.

"I'll take you to work and pick you up, if you'd like." Fonso parks in front of the cabin.

"Thanks, but I'll be okay. I'll take the bus. I want to clear my head before my shift."

A slow drizzle starts.

"Okay, but if it keeps raining, I'll take you if you want."

"Thank you."

Fonso goes inside. I sit on the porch and watch the slow fall of raindrops. I think of Dad and the water thickens. Some darker clouds move in. Colin pops into my head and thunder rolls. I stand. Pointing my hands toward the clouds, I send as much anger and negative thoughts as I can fathom. The woman who tried to grab me in New Orleans pops into my head. A bolt of lightning dashes between gray masses in the sky. I do it again, thinking of Kayla attacking me, the rage, resentment, and jealousy I felt. I wave my hand across the other direction and a bright white flash mimics me in the darkness.

Changing tactics, I remember the stargazing and the beauty of the planets through the telescope. I wipe the dirty clouds away, clearing the way for a brighter afternoon. The rain stops.

Deena comes out of the campground office. She waves when she sees me. I wave back.

Although emotions aren't always easy to control, at this moment, I discover thoughts carry more consistency. It's the simple remembrance of actions that allows me to change the weather in an instant.

"Hey." Fonso sticks his head out of the door. "Are you coming in?"

"Yeah. It's time to go to work, anyway."

"Say hello to Mr. Dreamy, and give him a kiss goodbye while you're at it." Fonso blows a kiss into the air.

"Yeah, I'm sure that'll happen." I give him a lopsided grin. "See you later." I grab my bag and head to the bus stop.

The bus driver smiles at me as I climb the steps. "I haven't picked anyone up here in a long time."

LIGHTNING STRUCK

My thoughts are jumbled on the ride to town. Events replay in my mind and I practice controlling my emotions to downplay them so the weather doesn't act up.

The bus stops at the place I first talked to Colin. I thank the driver and exit. Walking through town, I remember this morning and how Colin avoided looking at me. Was it possible he was ashamed of what he was doing? How can he be so awful to other people and be so good to me? He fixed a picnic lunch for me, for heaven's sake.

A gray cloud rolls in and I push it away, thinking about the bird pooping on Colin's head at the beach. That was unforgettable.

The diner's quiet as I enter.

"Hey stranger." Roger smiles at me.

"Hey."

"We've sure missed you the last two days." Roger nudges Abby. "Didn't we, hun?"

"Oh, yeah. It was pure hell here without you." Abby kicks Roger in the shin.

I laugh.

"Well, see you all later." Roger grabs Abby's hand and they leave. Outside, I see Roger bend down on the sidewalk and kiss Abby, and she smiles. It's the first time I've seen her smile.

"Hey." Kyle touches my shoulder and kisses me on the cheek. "How are you?"

"Good, and you?" I grab my pad. "Did you have a good day off?"

"It was uneventful." He shrugs. "What about you?"

"The same." I can't tell him I'm leaving. It dawns on me I don't want to leave. I only arrived days ago and I was just getting settled.

Kyle opens his mouth to say something, but the door dings as a couple of customers walk in. He rolls his eyes and goes to the kitchen.

Hours pass and the sprint of dinner customers dies down. It's only Kyle and me in the restaurant as I finish clearing and cleaning the last few tables. I pass the last of the dirty dishes through the window.

"Have you ever seen someone juggle kitchen utensils?" Kyle says as he grabs a spatula, a large spoon, and tongs, and attempts to juggle.

It ends horribly, but makes me laugh. "You've never tried out for the circus? Perhaps a clown school will take you."

"Hey, I think I'd look good in a bushy wig and red nose." Kyle crosses his eyes.

My smile doesn't leave for the rest of the night.

Roger walks in at eleven with one lagging customer at a table.

"I'll close up and finish the last table, Alice. You two have a good night."

Kyle rushes out of the kitchen and heads for the

door. Beating me to it, he holds it open for me. "Good night Roger."

"Good night Roger," I mimic in a deep voice.

"Good night you two. See you tomorrow." Roger chuckles.

It hits me I may not be here tomorrow and I'd be leaving him without coverage.

"What's wrong?" Kyle asks. "Smiling one minute and frowning another?"

"It's nothing." I fake a smile.

"Need a ride home?"

"Yes, please." I climb into his Jeep, thinking about the gun in the glove box. Is it still there?

"I was wondering if you'd like to go stargazing again tomorrow night? Supposed to be good weather." Kyle turns down my street.

"I, umm..." I hesitate.

"You don't want to?" The disappointment in his voice breaks me.

"I'd love to. I was trying to think if I promised anything to Fonso or not." I lie.

"Great. Can't wait." He beams.

Kyle drops me off in front of the cabin. He doesn't attempt to kiss me. I'm a bit relieved, yet disappointed.

"How did your night go?" Fonso asks. His pile of clothes is neatly stacked in a bag next to the couch. "I packed up your stuff, too. I left you out an outfit for tomorrow. I didn't have much else to do tonight."

It's time to tempt fate. I make a crucial decision, one Fonso may not like. "You can run with your family, but I'm not going. I'm tired of running." I sit on the couch, placing my legs up on the coffee table. "I'm staying right here and facing whatever it is that is coming for us...for me."

CHAPTER 17

"ARE YOU SURE you want to do this?" Fonso asks. "You'd be willing to stay on your own while we all pack up and leave?"

"You said the stones were a warning, right?"

"Yes." His expression hardens. "They want us gone."

"Why warn us then? Why not come and fight us and kill us if they are able to?"

"They have in the past. They took your dad, didn't they?"

"Yeah, and if they want to take me, too, then let them try." I cross my arms and rest my head back on the couch. "It won't be easy for them. I won't make it easy."

"You're either the bravest or stupidest Rom of all time." Fonso exhales.

"Stupidest? Is that even a word?" I laugh.

He shrugs. "Now, how are we not going to make this easy on 'them'?"

"We?" I ask.

"I'm not allowing you to stay by yourself to face whatever demons come. I can be as stubborn as you, too." He smiles. "Besides, I've been practicing."

"Your telekinesis?"

The refrigerator opens. A can of coke shoots through the air. Fonso catches it. "A little. It brings a whole new level to the term laziness."

We laugh.

"You can throw soda cans at them through the air. That'll be a big help."

"Whoever they are." Fonso's expression dulls. "You're sure about this?"

"Fonso, you don't have to stay with me because you feel like a protective big cousin. If you want to go with your family, I completely understand. I'm a big girl. Besides, I want to know what happened to Dad. I have a feeling I need to stay to figure it out."

"Maybe your gift is being stubborn."

I laugh again. "Maybe."

Someone knocks on the door.

Fonso lifts his eyebrows. His eyes grow as wide as beach balls. "I don't think it's for me."

"Elysia?" Colin's voice penetrates the wooden structure.

I stiffen when I hear the familiar voice. The voice

that told me kind words, and the one I heard growl to protect me. I ease off the couch. I was still angry at what I learned earlier today about his extortion business. With more curiosity then reluctance, I open the door and glare at him. "What do you want?" He's shirtless, his chest glistens with a thin layer of sweat.

He looks around me into the cabin, sees Fonso and glances at his packed bag. His eyes find mine. "You're mad at me." His voice is low and cautious.

I step from inside the cabin and invade his personal space, causing him to back up as I close the door behind me. Ignoring the electricity between us, I stand firm and lower my voice. "I saw you today. I saw you and you looked away from me, ashamed, and you should be. How can you do that to people?"

"Sometimes we have to do things we don't want to do." His eyes have a sadness in them I wasn't expecting.

He leans toward me. My heart rate quickens and my anger subsides, as it did at the beach or anytime he's near me. No matter the level of anger surging through me, he calms me. "You don't have to do the wrong thing, Colin. No matter what you feel you *need* to do. It's not right extorting innocent people."

He bends down and his lips touch mine. The urge to resist disappears and my mouth opens. He grabs me, pulling me to him. The kiss ignites a fire within me, as electricity pulses through my body. My hands slide down his tightening back muscles. The urge to throw him on the ground and ravage him scares me.

I push him away. "Stop."

"I'm sorry. I had to." He caresses my face with his fingers. "I had to kiss you once more."

He runs into the forest before I can say or do anything.

My knees weaken. I sit in the rocking chair.

Fonso peeks out the door. "He's not good for you, you know."

"Yes, I know. Don't you think I know that?" My heartbeat slows. "Every time I'm near him it becomes more and more difficult to tell him no."

"And Kyle?" He sits on the top step. "When you're around him, you don't feel that attraction?"

"It's different. Kyle is sweet, caring, and funny. Colin excites and scares me at the same time."

"You deliberately push Kyle away with trivial things that may not be a big deal, like the gun, but you're attracted to danger?"

"Not before now." I rock back and forth. Am I intentionally pushing Kyle away? With Colin, it's more than an attraction. It's like he tugs at part of my soul and I can't deny him.

Fonso stands. "I'm not sure what hold he has over you, but just be careful, okay?" He kisses the top of my head. "I'm going to bed. I have a feeling it's going to be a long day tomorrow."

"Good night." I turn toward the door. "Fonso?"

"Yeah?"

"Thank you for everything." I smile at him.

"Good night, Elysia."

***

"I'm going to town." Grabbing my bag from the counter.

Fonso rolls over on the couch. "What time is it?" He moans.

"It's just after seven."

"Why so early?"

"I've decided to be away from everyone in case they come looking for me. I don't like confrontations. You can tell them I'm not going."

"This from the person who's attracted to danger."

"Love ya." I blow kisses at him and leave the cabin.

Aunt Simza's truck and trailer are gone. Sadness tugs at my heart. The woman wanted nothing to do with me. And, although she didn't want me around, there must have been a reason I was sent to her. Fonso will be upset she lied to his family and left sometime in the night. Her word meant nothing. I wonder if he'll change his mind and go with them now.

"You're not leaving too, are you?" Deena asks

from her trailer stoop.

"No, I'm not leaving." I stop next to her trailer. "Going to town early, and then I have work later, but I'll be around."

"I don't know what I'll tell Madam Aishe's customers who come calling. I'm sure there will be lots." Deena twists her mouth to the side.

"Send them to Cassadaga."

"Where do you think they come from?" She rolls her eyes.

"I wish I had an answer for you. See you later." I continue to walk toward the bus stop.

The town is eerily quiet this early in the morning. I thought more people would be at the coffee shop before going to work, but there is only one other person in front of me. Sitting outside, sipping the fresh coffee, I glance around the small town square, it looks so peaceful.

"Not too many people out this morning." Emilian sits beside me at the table.

"What are you doing here? Shouldn't you be leaving?" I ask.

"Shouldn't you be?" His forehead furrows.

"I'm not one to follow orders."

"Seems to be catching, I guess." He leans back, pulling his chair on two legs. "Ma won't be too happy this morning when she realizes I'm gone, but she'll have Nadya and Fonso to keep her company. I was never much use to her anyway."

"What's that supposed to mean?"

"Well, Nadya finds things. Fonso is the smart one. I was always the one in trouble." He shrugs. "Not like they'd miss me much anyway."

"What are you going to do?" I ask. "Stay around town?"

"Don't worry. I'm not going to show up on your doorstep, begging for a place to stay or nothing." He watches the sun shine through the white clouds. "I have other friends."

"Like the friends that extort money from the townspeople?" I press my lips. "You're better than that, aren't you Emilian?"

"A lecture from you?" He chuckles. "That's ironic, seeing as you were kissing Colin last night."

"I—it wasn't..." My mouth hangs open, but I can't get a coherent thought out.

"Don't worry, I wasn't spying on you." He gives me a half-smile.

"It was a mistake."

"Your lips accidentally fell into his?"

"Fine. I don't have a right to tell you what to do." I close my eyes, taking a deep breath. "It was wrong to let him kiss me. He's not the person I thought he was."

"Did he tell you why he does it?" Emilian asks. "Why he and his friends take money from the locals?"

"No, he didn't say. There's no good reason to do any such thing. Are they so lazy that it's better to take than to work for the money?"

He ignores my question and stands. "They aren't as bad as you think they are. You don't know as much as you think you do."

A fleeting thought passes through my mind and I grab it before it disappears. "If you weren't spying on me then what were you doing?"

"I was helping Aunt Simza."

"You knew she wouldn't keep to her word, didn't you?" He shrugs and starts to walks away. "Emilian."

He stops and faces me.

"Go with your family. They do need you and they love you." I plead, wondering if he's even told them he's not going with them.

"The last time Ma told me she loved me was when I was seven and broke my arm. Instead of taking me to a hospital, she made one of the carnies patch it up. She said, 'I love you Emilian, but I can't afford no hospital.'" He bends his arm and the elbow jerks. "It never healed right. That was the last time she said she loved me and it came with a but."

He stares at me. I nod. My heart aches for him. It's hard to believe Aunt Mirela would be so callous, but people get wrapped up in themselves, and taking care of others, they forget the truly important things in life. In her own way, I'm sure she loves all her children, but maybe she has difficulty showing it. Not only to Emilian, but also to Fonso and Nadya.

It makes me think about how my grandfather treated his three daughters, including my mother. I wonder how she would have been to me had she lived. Dad was loving and caring, although a bit overbearing and protective.

I walk for hours around town, and I can't get what Emilian said out of my head. What did he mean by, *"They aren't as bad as you think they are."*

Still coming up with no answers, I visit the small wildlife refuge, and try to clear the confusing thoughts before I head into work.

"You're early." Roger smiles when I walk in.

"I didn't have much else to do." I wipe down the counter bar area.

"Do you want something to eat?" Roger offers. "It's on me."

My stomach growls as if on cue. "Sure."

"Sit down then. No reason to help now. We ain't got much to do." Abby sets a place at the counter for me to sit.

"Okay." No customers are in the diner. "Has it been slow?"

"Yeah, some festival going on by the beach. Most folks take off to go." Roger places water down for me. "Want some ice tea or soda?"

"Unsweetened tea, please."

"You're not from the South, that's for sure." Abby pours the tea. "If you were, you'd be having the sweet stuff."

"I drink it both ways, but I prefer unsweetened."

"I think that's illegal in most states." She laughs and Roger joins in. Abby seems to be warming up to me in her own twisted way.

"What'll you have?" Roger asks.

"One of Sam's burgers." I lick my lips.

Kyle sticks his head through the window. "Aren't my burgers good enough?"

Roger slaps his knees, chuckling loudly.

"Okay Roger, it wasn't that funny. Calm down before you give yourself a heart attack." Abby warns. "Let's go early since they are both here. No customers are here and Kyle can fix Alice a burger."

"All right Abby. You win." He grabs her purse and gives it to her. "See you kids later."

"Good night." Abby waves.

I move my setting behind the counter in case customers come in.

"Have you even tried my burger?" Kyle asks. "I don't think you have."

"I haven't. Should I be scared?" I grin. "I hear it's not as good as Sam's."

"You should be very scared." The burger sizzles when he squashes it down.

"What are you doing here this early?" I ask.

"Sam needed the day off. He's going to the festival. I should have asked you to go, but I promised I'd cover for Sam."

"That was nice of you."

He serves the burger through the window with fries on the plate. "I can be nice sometimes."

The door bell chimes. Aunt Mirela and Nadya walk in.

"Why are you doing this to me?" Aunt Mirela cries out.

"I'm not doing anything to you." I rush around the counter to stop them from coming in further. "I'm not going."

"You and Fonso and, now, Emilian. You come into town and turn my boys against me?"

Nadya grabs her mom's shaking shoulders. "Ma, it's not Alice's fault."

"Elysia. Her name's Elysia." Aunt Mirela nods, her voice rising. "That's right. We know you lied about your name. Simza knows your name. Maybe that's why she doesn't trust you. You're a liar. What else did you lie about?"

Kyle walks from the kitchen. I hold my hand up and wave him to leave. He stops but doesn't leave the seating area. Heat rises inside me. "Did she tell you why I'm here?" I whisper. "Did she tell you they took my father?"

"If they took Harman, that's his fault." Aunt Mirela spits. "He hid you away from all of us. Maybe he deserved to be taken."

Nadya moves her hands from her Aunt Mirela's shoulders and backs up. She's visibly shaken.

"How dare you!" The thunder roars outside. "How dare you! My father is a good man and did what he thought was right to protect us. No one deserves to be hunted down like a dog. No one."

"This is all your fault. I see why Simza wants nothing to do with you." Aunt Mirela turns, grabs Nadya's hand and pulls her out of the diner.

"What's going on?" Kyle asks as he comes up behind me.

A tear falls down my cheek and I choke back a sob. He turns me in his arms and embraces me.

"Family problems, is all."

His arms feel warm. He kisses the top of my head. "I guess we have that in common, too."

I smile into his shoulder.

The diner remains empty all night.

"Are you still up for stargazing tonight?" Kyle stands with a dish towel over his shoulder, watching the rain fall in the darkness outside. "Maybe the rain will stop and it'll clear up. Either way, the weatherman should be shot."

"It would be nice to be under the stars again."

"I'll empty the trash for Roger, since it's slow.

Get me if someone comes in." He walks toward the back door.

While he's gone, I think of the last time we went stargazing. Seeing the clusters through the telescope was magical. The rain slows into a drizzle and stops.

A clang echoes through the back door. I run across the kitchen. Stepping out the back door, the first thing I see is Colin swinging at Kyle.

CHAPTER 18

THUNDER BOOMS OVERHEAD. A grayish whirl forms in the sky. I'm the only one who sees it.

Colin hits Kyle. Kyle retaliates, punching Colin in the face.

"Stop!" I yell. They ignore my plea.

They circle each other, kicking and punching. Then, Colin grabs Kyle by the neck.

I scream. The whirl in the sky rotates faster.

Roger runs through the back door and grabs Kyle, pushing Colin off him. He twists him around, hurrying him and me back into the diner.

He faces Colin. "I paid you this week. Leave us alone." He slams the door.

Roger grabs his chest. "Are you kids all right? Kyle, are you hurt?"

"I'm fine, Roger." He dabs a dishcloth against his busted lip. "This wasn't your fault." He throws the rag into the sink. "It was my fault." He stares at me.

"He's not supposed to be anywhere around here." Roger locks the back door. "We have an agreement."

"You pay him." My emotions waiver. My thoughts and feelings are almost impossible to control. "You pay him every week, don't you Roger?"

He nods.

"Why?"

"I don't want to talk about it." Roger rushes past. "You and Kyle can go." He looks at Kyle. "Make sure she gets home safe."

Kyle nods.

Kyle presses me to leave. I grab my bag and walk out the front door with him on my heels.

"What's going on?" I ask. "What happened?"

"Ask Colin. He seems to know you much better than I do." Kyle opens the door, a frown on his reddened face.

"I'm asking you."

The rain starts before he gets into the driver's seat. "He was waiting for me in the alley."

"Why?"

"He warned me to stay away from you." Kyle starts the Jeep, gunning it out of the parking lot. "He made it clear you two were intimate and you want nothing to do with me."

"He what?" Anger boils within me. Does Colin

171

think he owns me?

He pulls off to the side of the road. "I didn't realize he was taking money from Roger." He bangs his steering wheel. "Of all the people...why him? He doesn't deserve this."

"He doesn't." Tears fall. I can't stop them. The rain descends steadily. Everything in the last week has gotten so out of control: my emotions, family, impulses.

He turns his attention to me. "I'm sorry." He grabs my hand. "Don't cry. It's not your fault. He's a thief and a liar."

"Take me home, please." I sniffle, embarrassed to have broken down in front of him.

"Okay." He pulls the Jeep onto the road. His hand holds mine the entire way home.

When we arrive, I notice Fonso's car is missing.

"Let me come in with you."

I nod.

My hand trembles as I turn the key. I glance at the couch and see Fonso's bag still there. Relief floods me. He would have taken his stuff had he left...wouldn't he?

"Do you have tequila?" Kyle asks.

"Yes, in the cupboard by the fridge." I throw my bag on the counter. "I'm going to the bathroom."

When I return, he has a shot ready for me. We sit on the couch. He holds me while we listen to the rain.

"It wouldn't have been great weather for stargazing anyway." He pulls me close.

"I'm sorry about everything that happened tonight. It wasn't a good day for me." I lean into him and allow myself to be comforted.

"There'll be better days." He kisses the top of my head. "Elysia."

"You caught that?" I shy away.

"It was hard not to with her rant." He pulls me back. "Why did you lie about your name?"

"Maybe I'd rather be an Alice."

"Elysia is a beautiful name." Hearing my real name come from his lips is surreal.

"Thank you."

"But you were also so comfortable with Alice."

"I'm used to changing my name." The truth feels good.

"You're so mysterious." He gets up and refills our shot glasses. "Why do you do that? Are you in the witness relocation program?"

I smile. "Not likely. We moved around a lot; my father and I. Didn't you ever want to pretend to be someone else?"

"I never thought about it. I guess there were times I wished I had a different life or a career path. Yes, I've often wanted to be someone else."

"Changing my name helped me pretend to be someone else. A clean slate. Only now, I don't want to do it any more. Hearing you call me Elysia is nice."

"Did you turn her sons against her?"

"She's delusional and blaming me for her shortcomings. Maybe my independence ignited an already strong desire in my cousins to seek theirs."

"I think you bring out the best in people." He interweaves his fingers in with mine.

"I doubt that. I tend to bring only storms and heartache."

"That's not true."

"Thank you for the shot." I gulp it down; the tension in my body subsides. "And thank you for staying to comfort me."

"Thank you for letting me." He leans and kisses me. It's soft and sweet.

He stays until I can no longer keep my eyes open. He tucks me into bed and kisses me on the forehead. I hear the front door open and close as he leaves. I'm not sure I wanted him to until my thoughts drift to Colin and a calm settles over me. I fall asleep, listening to the rain patter against the cabin roof.

***

Clattering from the kitchen wakes me.

I walk into the living room. "What is going on in here?"

LIGHTNING STRUCK

Fonso stops messing with a pot on the stove. Nadya is sitting on the couch next to a bag of clothes.

"Oh no." I shake my head.

Nadya frowns. A tear falls down her cheek. "I think I'm the reason your father's missing."

CHAPTER 19

A STATIC RINGING in my ears blocks out my cousin's words as she opens her mouth. The room spins. A dark blanket covers my eyes.

"Elysia. Elysia." Fonso holds a cold cloth on my forehead.

"What..." An eerie dimness covers the room. Rain beats against the cabin and thunder booms.

"The lights went out. I think a bolt hit the transformer." Fonso dabs my flushed cheeks. "You fainted."

Nadya hugs her knees in the corner chair. Dark streaks of mascara run down her face. "I'm so sorry. I didn't know."

I sit up. The back of my head throbs. "That hurts." I feel the back of my head and a bump is starting to form.

"You hit your head when you fell. I couldn't

catch you in time." Fonso helps me up. "It's not Nadya's fault, Elysia. She didn't know what she was doing."

An explosion rumbles above.

Nadya opens her mouth. I hold up a finger to stop her words from forming.

I breathe deeply and concentrate on my emotions, imagining the clouds rolling away and the clear sky blossoming in its wake. The rain and thunder begin to subside. I breathe in and out a few more times. "You said you're the reason my father's missing. What did you mean?"

Fonso sits next to me and hands me the cold cloth. I place it on the forming bump.

"Yesterday, when Ma and I went to the diner—"

"Yes. She was angry with me. No fault of my own, by the way."

"She mentioned your dad's name was Harman." Nadya pauses.

"Yes, that's his name." I widen my eyes.

"His last name is Lovell?" The side of her mouth curves up.

"Yes. My dad's name is Harman Lovell. Go on."

"For as long as I can remember, Ma asked me at least once a year to locate a man named Harman Lovell. She said it was for a client and would help us. I didn't question her for a long time. She had asked me to locate people before, but that name came up more often than any other." She clears her scratchy throat. "I was beginning to think he was a ghost because he's the only one she would ask me about continuously. I kept wondering why they hadn't found him yet. Last year I asked her why. She insisted he was a druggie and often ran away."

"My aunt?" Betrayal is a new feeling; one I don't like.

Clunks of ice hitting the wooden boards cause a moment of silence.

"It's hailing. Have you ever seen weather this strange in your life? Can it even hail in Florida?" Fonso shakes his head.

"She never asked about you," Nadya ignores her brother and continues, "She was as surprised as we were when you showed up. I honestly think she didn't know you existed."

"Every year?" I ask. "She made you try to find him every year?"

Nadya nods.

"We had to move often because the Hunters always seemed to find us." I lean back, placing my head on the cloth and the back of the couch. "Dad always knew they were coming. That was his gift. He knew trouble was coming."

"Why didn't he leave this time, then? Why did he get caught?" Fonso asks.

"The morning he came to get me, he seemed

different. He was tense and frantic. I didn't understand, I thought we were happy in Baton Rouge. But, he waited too long." My thoughts jumble together. "I know he was tired of running, but he wouldn't risk me being caught, so he made me flee alone."

"Baton Rouge," she says in a hushed voice. "That's where I told Ma to look." Her eyes meet mine for the first time. "I led them right to him." Nadya's voice rises. "The year before that, I led them to South Carolina. The year before Buffalo, New York."

"Those were all places we lived." I rise. The hail subsides. I stand at the window and look out at the seemingly desolate campground. "Why would Aunt Mirela betray us? Why would she work with the Hunters?"

"Money?" Fonso asks. "Money is the root of all evil. We've always been in a weak position. There've been times Ma didn't have any work, even at the carnival. Not everyone is interested in knowing their past."

"I guess so." Nadya curls back up in a ball.

"Did you tell Aunt Mirela you were leaving?" I ask. "She must be even more pissed at me."

"I went to get her last night. Ma threw a fit. I've never heard so much screaming in my life," Fonso says.

"I was worried when I didn't see your car when I

got home." I sigh. "She knew what she did to Dad from the moment she met me and said nothing. She didn't bat an eyelash as she invited me into her home and introduced me to her family. All that time, she knew they had Dad."

"Maybe she didn't know." Nadya looks at me. "You didn't say anything to her about him missing until yesterday and she must have known about his gift."

"I'm so mad." The thunder rolls outside.

Fonso turns on the TV. The weatherman talks about a low chance of rain and nice sunny weather. "The science of meteorology sucks. They have no freaking idea what they're talking about." He glances out the window. "They'd be better off just looking up instead of depending on all that scientific crap."

I smile. I breathe and think about the beach: the waves crashing against the shore, hoping to calm the churning and relentless storms outside.

I see Deena run from her camper to the campground office. I've forgotten to pay her and she's too nice to come and get it. "I'll be back."

The clouds evaporate above me. I feel pride at learning to control my ever changing emotions. These last couple of weeks have tested me.

"Hi Alice." Deena smiles when I enter. "How are you?"

I place two week's rent on the counter. "I'm fine.

I'm sorry I didn't come yesterday."

"I know where you live, so that's not a problem." She winks. "How's your cousin? Did he find another job?"

"He did." I turn to walk out and without thinking I ask, "Deena, have you ever felt lost?"

"Somehow I knew you'd ask me that." She comes out from behind the counter and stands in front of me. "Once, when I was a little girl, my uncle wanted to take my two brothers and me on a hike. We were camping at a state park filled with tall pines by a canal. Gators were everywhere back then. We went on this hike with him. He was part Native American, and maybe he had a point to prove, I don't know, but he took us off the known trail. We hiked for hours in deep brush. Our ankles were all cut up from the rough palmettos, and the insects were something horrible. It was late. My younger brothers and I were hungry, thirsty, and tired...too stubborn to admit it though, as my uncle was too stubborn to declare he was lost."

"What did you do?"

"He finally acknowledged he got us lost. My brother suggested he climb a tree to see where we were. Such a simple thought and it came from the youngest in the group. Had my uncle not admitted he was lost, my brother might not have suggested it. My uncle climbed the nearest pine tree and saw where we were and where we needed to go."

"That's a neat story, but not what I meant by lost." I smile.

"I know. It wasn't so much about the story as it was about the message. Whenever you are lost, sometimes you need others to show you the way." She rubs my back. "We all get lost from time to time. We stray from a path; have to overcome obstacles. It's tougher when you do it alone. Trust me, I know. Well, at least I like to think I do." She baulks out a laugh. "Hell, child, I thrive on a challenge, hence why I'm alone."

An idea forms as I thank Deena.

I run back to the cabin and throw the door open.

"What?" Nadya jumps. "You scared the crap out of me."

"You're going to help me find my father."

CHAPTER 20

ONSO AND I wait outside. I peek through the window to see Nadya meditating as she faces the wall; finding a specific person isn't easy for her, apparently.

"I didn't realize it would be so difficult." I rock in the chair on the porch. "It always seemed so easy for her to find things and people. She found my job, Roger's keys—even found us at the mall."

"It's easier for her to find things, or people she's close with, but finding complete strangers is different. It took her a week to find a missing person for one of Ma's clients, but she ended up being dead." Fonso uses his gift to launch pine cones into the air and smacking them against a tree.

"That's not helping."

"She's located him before so it won't be too hard for her...I hope." He tries to levitate a large log.

"What if Deena or someone else sees you doing

that?"

"She won't. And besides, I need to practice."

"Aren't you supposed to start your new job soon?" I lean against the wooden railing.

"Yesterday." He gives a lopsided grin.

"That's nice."

"There was a lot going on yesterday. I didn't know what would happen."

"I have to go to work today. I need to talk to Roger and see Kyle." I peek in the window. Nadya is still meditating in the corner. "Will you call me as soon as you...as soon as she finds him?"

He nods.

"And practice around back so no one will see you accidently move a trailer or cabin with your mind. I can't bare to bring another person into this crazy world of ours."

"Do you want me to drive you into town?"

I shake my head. "Stay with Nadya. I'll catch the bus."

"Alright."

***

Abby's behind the register cashing out a customer. Roger sees me, shakes his head and lifts his finger to his lips as he nods toward Abby. He doesn't want her to find out about last night.

LIGHTNING STRUCK

I watch through the kitchen window as Sam turns over the kitchen to Kyle for the night shift.

"Alice." Abby gives me a half-smile.

"Abby." I clean the newly-emptied table. Abby goes into the back. It's now or never. "Roger, I want to talk to you."

"Can't it wait till later?" He avoids eye contact.

"Why are you paying them? Why not go to the police?" I whisper. "You don't need to do it."

"Not now." Roger pats me on the back.

Abby emerges from the back with her purse. "You coming?"

"I'm coming. Hold your britches." Roger forces a smile.

They leave and I throw the dishes into the tub in the kitchen.

"What did those dishes ever do to you?" Kyle asks.

"They're being extorted and used and they refuse to do anything about it." I huff. "Did you talk with him?" I turn to see Kyle, purple surrounding his right, puffy eye.

"No. He wouldn't talk to me, either." Kyle flips a turkey burger. "Some people came in."

"Kyle. I'm sorry about your eye."

"No big deal. I'm sure I got some good hits in, too."

I return to the front of the diner and wait on the

newcomers.

In-between customers, I stand by the phone, hoping Fonso will call and tell me Nadya found Dad.

"Did you want to go out tonight?"

Kyle's voice causes me to jump.

"I didn't mean to startle you." Kyle puts his hands on my shoulders. "You're on edge."

"I can't tonight. My cousin, Nadya, is staying at my cabin and I need to get home to make sure it's still in one piece."

"Now you have two cousins there? Isn't it getting crowded?"

"You have no idea."

"Are you mad at me for not staying with you last night?" Kyle lowers his hands and leans against the archway. His white shirt clings to his torso, revealing his Herculean chest.

"No, not at all. It was nice you stayed with me for as long as you did." I lower my head. "I must seem like the ultimate basket case."

"You did ask, you know." He grins sheepishly.

"I asked you to stay?"

He takes two long strides to me and wraps me in his arms. "You asked me to stay the night with you."

"I did not. I think I'd remember something like that."

"You did. Granted, you were practically asleep at the time, but it was a definite invitation." He pulls me closer, leaning against the wall.

"I think you were dreaming."

"Too bad I woke up, then." He bends to kiss me, but the bell disturbs us. Two customers come in and have a seat in the far booth against the window.

The diner clears. The phone hasn't rung once so I have no idea if Nadya found Dad or not. I tap my nails on the counter over and over again. "Kyle, tell me about your last relationship. How did she ever let you go?" I don't know what made me blurt out the question.

"She didn't have a choice." Kyle hangs clean pots on the racks above his head. "She was one of the biggest bitches you'd ever meet. I do not say that lightly."

I laugh. "Then why did you go out with her?"

"Why are we talking about this?" he asks with a twinge of curiosity in his tone.

"Because I want to know how someone was so lucky to catch you and then so unlucky to lose you."

He laughs and clutches his chest. "So, what you're saying is I'm a great catch?"

I smirk. "Just answer the question."

"She wasn't always awful. She had her sweet moments, but she became so consumed."

"Consumed with what?"

"Work."

"Oh, those types of career driven women aren't

your style?"

"Not even close." He leans through the window and kisses me.

"You broke it off because she became consumed with her work?"

"That's it in a nutshell." He washes his hands. "We grew in different directions. She wanted one thing and I was looking to start a carefree lifestyle."

"Was it serious?"

"It was." He nods. "It's now seriously over. What about you?"

"I've never been serious in a relationship. There's been crushes, but nothing that lasted too long."

"Their loss is my gain." Kyle wiggles his eyebrows.

Eleven o'clock nears. My feet ache. I walked too much yesterday and coupled with the stress, exhaustion hits me hard. I could use a good massage and bubble bath, but neither is likely to happen. "Do you need help back there?"

"Nah, I've got it," Kyle yells from the rear. "Almost done."

I sneak back to scare him...to see if I can get him to jump as he did earlier to me.

He's on his phone. "No, I haven't discovered the pack leader, yet. I think Colin is hiding him."

CHAPTER 21

KYLE'S EYES WIDEN when he sees me standing behind him. "I can explain." The screen on his phone goes black and he shoves it in his pocket.

I raise my hand. "No!"

I dash out of the diner, past Roger, and into the dark parking lot.

Heading toward the bus stop, I look back to see Kyle running out of the diner. He spots me. I run faster.

Colin is leaning against his truck. He has one foot propped up against the running board. He seems so far at the other end of the street, but with Kyle trailing me, I run as fast as I can toward him. He stiffens when he sees me.

I run to the passenger side. "Can you give me a ride?" I ask, out of breath.

"Elysia!" Kyle yells. "Don't!"

"Jump in." Colin climbs into his truck.

I do. As I fasten my seatbelt, I turn to see Kyle stop on the opposite side of the street. He kicks a trach can as Colin takes off.

"Thank you." I lean against the cloth headrest.

"You're welcome." His voice is deep and edged with concern.

"Don't think I've forgiven you for what happened yesterday, or even the day before, or even—" I don't finish as I cross my arms. "Why did you do it? Why did you tell Kyle we were intimate and together and warn him away from me? Why are you extorting money from Roger? He's the nicest man around and doesn't deserve it." The questions rolled off my tongue as if I had planned this moment. I didn't, but I didn't stop. "If you take even one more penny from him again, I'll kick your ass myself. Don't think I can't do it, because I can." I rattle on, anger fueling me.

The sky should be fuming along with me, but it's not. Colin reaches out and unwraps my arms. He gently holds my hand within his. Why does his touch always bring me the comfort I need?

"Where are we going?" We weave down a dirt road I'm not familiar with.

He doesn't answer.

He parks his truck at a dead end. "Come on." He pulls me through the driver's side door.

LIGHTNING STRUCK

A frog croaks, then another. Colin leads me through a maze of trees with overhanging moss to a dock. A canoe is tied to the end of it. "You're taking me on the water? If you're planning to kill me and feed me to the gators, you should know, I don't taste that great. I'm sure of it."

"Would you shut up?" He pulls me to him, igniting the electricity between us, and kisses me deeply.

All the anger melts away between us. My head grows fuzzy, and I have a momentary memory lapse of why I was angry with him. Our lips part. He places his forehead against mine.

"Come on." He pulls me down the dock and helps me into the canoe. "No one will bug us out here. Except maybe the mosquitoes."

I have no choice but to face him in the canoe. "Do you think every time I'm mad at you that you can kiss me and everything will be fine?"

He unties it and paddles away from the dock. "Would you like me to stop kissing you?"

No. No. No. I turn, but say nothing.

The three-quarters moon illuminates the rippling water. Two red eyes dive below the surface. Flying bugs skim the water as if dancing on it, reminding me of fairies sliding across a lake I'd seen in a childhood cartoon. A musty scent, like a mixture of mud and damp wood, assails my nostrils. Crickets and frogs play a melody on the water's edge. Hearing the paddle as it ripples through the water reminds me of a babbling brook.

"Will you answer my questions now?" I softly ask the wind.

"Jealousy." He moves the paddle over, and a few water droplets fly to meet my back. "I told Kyle to stay away from you because I was jealous."

"You told him we were intimate."

"To me, our kisses are intimate." He stops paddling. "They are special. Don't you feel it?"

I did, but I'm too stubborn to say it aloud.

"Kyle is a good guy." I think. Hearing him on the phone talking about Colin and his pack makes me think I don't know him as well as I thought. But, my gut tells me he means well; even if he does have other intentions.

"He's the wrong guy for you." Colin paddles on the left to avoid an overhanging branch.

"That's not for you to decide."

"You're right. It's not." His voice tightens. "I shouldn't have acted like a crazed, obsessive dick."

The stars are bright and there's not a cloud in sight. I do a mental scan and realize I'm completely calm.

He steers further down the bank and drifts into an alcove. He jumps from the canoe, shaking it. I gasp in a breath. "I've got you." Colin ties the canoe to a tree and helps me to the bank. He leads me inland to a spot under a large oak tree and unfolds a blanket.

I sit and hesitantly lie back. I look up through the moss hanging in the branches to see the moon and stars twinkling. I feel the heat from his body as he lies next to me. A shiver runs through me as he presses closer and wraps his arms around me. "Do you accept my apology?" he whispers.

"What are you apologizing for?"

His shadowy face blocks my view. "Everything." He kisses me. His right arm slides behind me, cradling me. His left hand follows my curvy side, leaving sparks in its wake.

A moan escapes my lips. A fire burns inside me that only he can extinguish.

All my worries fade away, replaced with a wicked longing; a desire I've never felt in all my life overtakes me. I need to have him. My body aches for him to do more than caress me.

A frisson runs through me and Colin trembles. I pull his shirt off. He kisses my jawline and moves down to my neck, a pulsing sensation follows the trail of his lips.

Nothing in the world matters more than this moment, us together, joining as one. My fingers feel numb as if the storm is happening inside of me and needs to be released.

We lie with each other for minutes, hours...all

track of time vanishes.

The moon watches over us; the tree protects us; the moss fans us.

I rest my head on his bare chest, listening to his heartbeat slow. "You're forgiven," I whisper.

He laughs and brings my hand to his lips and kisses it.

A howl erupts in the distance. His body tenses underneath me.

"What is it?"

"They're calling me."

"Don't go. Please stay with me."

"For you...anything." He relaxes. "I can't explain it, even though I know I should go—I'm supposed to go—for the first time in my life I can resist the call."

I prop my head up. "When we are together, you comfort me. Even when I'm so angry that I feel as though I could crush buildings, you calm me. I can't explain it."

"Why are you still here, though?" His expression turns serious.

"Huh? What do you mean?"

"I sent the stones to protect you; to protect your family. You shouldn't be here still." He pushes me up. "Something worse is coming to town and as much as I want you to stay, you need to leave."

Suddenly, the puzzle pieces seem more scattered. "You sent the stones?"

"Yes." Colin rises, tugging me up with him. "If you could stay safe with me in this moment forever, I would want nothing else, but the reality of the situation is you need to get out of town with your family."

The sun's morning rays beam through a string of clouds on the horizon. I gasp. "We've been here all night. My cousins must be freaking out."

"Here, call them." He hands me his phone.

"It's going to voice mail."

"Leave a message." Colin dresses, handing me my shirt.

"Fonso, it's me. I'm okay. I'm sorry I didn't call sooner. Something came up. Call me back at this number." I hang up and hand Colin back his phone. "Thank you."

"You're welcome." He tosses me my jeans. "We need to get going."

"What's coming?"

He shakes the dirt off the blanket, wrapping it up in a ball. "The packs are coming."

"Packs? As in multiple?"

"As in the powerful ones. As in too many to hide you from." Colin helps me into the canoe.

"Why do you need to hide us? I don't understand."

He pushes off from the bank. "They aren't friendly to Gypsies. They despise them."

"You've been fine with Emilian."

"We're different. Riley, Brayden, Kayla, and I see things, we don't feel the hate our kind generally does. We're natural enemies, Elysia. Werewolves harbor an instinctive need to eliminate your kind."

"Eliminate? Like you want to kill us?"

"We know about your abilities. Your kind sees things, they can do things. Emilian knew exactly what we were when he first saw us. His sister finds things. His aunt talks to the dead. These things are threats to my kind."

"Emilian told you all of this?"

He nods. "He also told us you have no ability, but I think he's wrong."

My stomach turns.

"The way that I'm attracted to you. The effect you have on me...you must be a siren." He smiles. "Look at Kyle. He's hooked on you, too. Don't deny it."

It's a miracle no one here has figured out the weather is wacky whenever I'm around and can't control my emotions. Kayla almost died because of it, and he thinks I'm a siren? I laugh. "I promise you, I'm no siren."

"There's a theory the younger Gypsies don't have abilities; like they are being bred out of them. Makes sense to us, since our werewolf gene isn't passed down to everyone, either."

"My father was taken by the Hunters. Do you

know anything about that?"

"No. When did this happen?"

My gut instinct tells me he's being honest. I give him the short story and why I'm here. He listens intently. When the sadness comes, clouds form overhead, but they don't betray me. They hover, waiting for me to give the order.

"I don't think it was my kind that did it. They're impulsive, aggressive and unsteady, but not calculating enough to hold hostages." He pauses. "You're sure he's still alive?"

"He's alive. I feel it. I think my aunt knows where he is or who has him."

"The one who talks to the dead?" He ties the canoe up, helping me out.

"No. Aunt Mirela. Emilian's mom." I become angry and a boom cracks in the distance. "We believe she was paid to tell someone Dad's location over the years."

"Let's go. We need to get you and your cousins out of town today. I don't know when the others will arrive, but it'll be soon. I hope they're not already here."

Colin drives slowly through the town. He watches every movement, glancing down alleyways, and constantly staring in his rearview mirror. Even when we hit the road heading toward the campground and my aunt's place, he can't take his eyes from the woods on either side.

Sitting close to him, I rest my head on his shoulder. "This can't be it. Am I supposed to leave and never see you again?"

His phone vibrates. "It's Riley. I'll text him in a minute." He places the phone on his lap and grabs my hand. "I don't want you to leave me, either. It's better this way, though."

He pulls into my aunt's place. It's empty. No cars line the driveway.

Colin parks and helps me down from his truck. He runs around to the back of the doublewide trailer, while I look in the windows. The furniture remains, but all the trinkets are gone. The door's locked.

I sit on the stoop.

Colin appears in front of me. "There's no trace of them." He texts someone. "Emilian is with Brayden and them. He's a damn fool. Why didn't he leave with his mother?"

"Is he?" I rub my temple. "Don't you get tired of running?"

"We aren't the runners, Elysia. We're the chasers." He sits next to me. "But, yes, I'm tired of this game. I'm tired of all of it."

"Why do you take money from Roger and the other shop owners?"

"None of us want to." Colin hangs his head. "My father gives orders and we can't ignore them."

"Your father?"

"He's our pack leader. He sent us here to secure the area a year ago. We were hoping he'd let us live alone, away from the larger pack. No such luck. He called a few days ago."

"What if you run away? With me?"

"It's not that easy. We're bound to his will. It's hard to explain."

"This is unbearable."

His phone vibrates again. He glances at it and hands it to me.

"It's Fonso." I put it on speaker. "Fonso, I'm so sorry. I'll be home soon."

"Good. We thought the Hunters had gotten you. That wasn't cool, Elysia." He pauses. "Am I on speaker? Who's phone is this?"

"It's Colin's."

Colin walks toward his truck.

"Wonderful. Take me off speaker."

"What's going on?"

"Nadya thinks she's found your father."

CHAPTER 22

I'M JOLTED FORWARD as something rams into the back of Colin's truck as we begin to back out.

"What the fuck?" Colin's arm flies out to protect me from hitting my head.

I look out the back window to see Kyle's Jeep behind us. "Why is he doing this?"

Colin jumps down, raging madness etched on his face. "We don't have time for this. Move that piece of shit and get out of our way!" he yells at Kyle.

I climb out of the truck. Kyle circles away from his Jeep, coming closer to Colin.

"He's not who you think, Elysia." He yanks his gun out, pointing it at Colin.

Thunder roars.

"You've lost it, Kyle. She knows exactly what I am." Colin grabs me and shoves me behind him. The moment he touches me, the thunder subsides.

It's Colin. His touch—his body—being near him

stabilizes my abilities.

"Elysia, step away from him. You're not going to believe this, but—"

"He's a werewolf." I move under Colin's arm, standing in front of him. "And you're looking for his pack leader. I heard you on the phone last night."

"I knew there was something off with you. You've always had it out for me. Even in class when we'd fight I felt that aggression." Colin tries to move me back, but I push him away. "Put the gun down. You're pointing it at her."

Kyle aims it toward the ground. "Yes, I've had it out for you. I knew what you were the minute I set eyes on you."

"How did you know?" I ask. "Why are you after them?"

"He killed my mother." A tear forms in the corner of his eye. "He and his kind killed her in cold blood."

Colin stiffens.

"I wanted to kill you the first time I saw you in town." Kyle's jaw tightens. "I couldn't because we needed to know who the pack leader calling the shots was." He raises his gun again. "Who is it?"

"I'm sure Colin didn't kill your mother." Colin paces near me; his body trembles. "Right, Colin?" I touch his arm and his body calms.

Kyle pulls out a picture from his back pocket, throwing it on the ground. It's a security camera picture of Colin near a woman's body. He's naked, blood dripping from his mouth.

"Oh, God." Bile rises in my throat.

"Her name was Sonya." Colin drops to the ground, squatting. "She was my first and only kill. He made me do it. I had no choice. I had to prove myself." Remorse is laced throughout his words.

"Oh, God." I clench my stomach.

Colin stands. He grips my hips and looks into my eyes. "She was Rom. She could manipulate thoughts...make people do things they wouldn't normally do." His eyes water.

I shake my head as I stare at him with disbelief.

Kyle's eyes bore into Colin. "Do you know the restraint it's taken not to kill you these last few months?"

I've never seen this side of Kyle. His anger and hatred turn him into an entirely different person.

"You ripped her throat out and left her there. She didn't deserve it. She didn't deserve to be attacked by some wild, raging animal. That's what you are. You're a fucking beast."

Colin faces him. His back is to me as he tucks me behind him. "Kill me, then. Will that make you feel better? I won't even try to run. And, to make it easy on you, I even agree with you, I deserve it. But, if think I enjoyed that?" He points to the picture. "Then you are sadly mistaken."

"No!" I wedge between them, holding my arms up. My hand covers the gun barrel.

"You still take his side?" Kyle lowers his gun. "After you've seen what he did?"

My heart aches for them both. It starts to rain; this time, I want it to.

"Who's the pack leader?" Kyle asks Colin, raindrops dripping down his face.

"My father. He's the one who gave the order. He wanted your mother dead." Colin grabs my hand. "All of us, the entire pack, follow his orders, or the consequences are severe."

"I'm part Rom; does he want me dead, too?" Kyle asks.

"I don't sense a trace of Rom blood in you. If we had, you'd already be dead."

The gun shakes in Kyle's hand. "We've been tracking your kind for years and killing every one we find. Did you know that?" he asks. "My dad sent me here on a hunch, and I found you. You're all I wanted. After you and your father, I'm done with your kind. I don't care about the rest of you dogs."

"You've been killing innocents, then. The lone wolves don't belong to a pack. If you tried to kill a pack member, you wouldn't be standing here talking to me." Colin wipes his face. "Even the best predators don't stand a chance against a pack of werewolves."

"You were sent here?" I ask Kyle.

203

"My father knew your family was in the area," Kyle explains. "Where there are Roma, there are usually werewolves close by." He bites his lip and his body trembles. "I didn't mean to—you weren't supposed to get involved, Elysia."

"Your father knows my family?" I ask. "Is that why you wanted to go out with me? To get close to my family?"

"I liked you because from the first moment I saw you, I was attracted to you. I imagined a future with you, a life outside of this crazy, revenge-seeking life I've been living for years."

"I trusted you, and you lied to me. What happened to the free-spirited, easy-going lifestyle?"

"The moment you walked into the diner, I wanted to shut the entire world out, forget about werewolves, my father's orders, and my mother's death. You made me want to forget all of it. There's something special about you." He steps forward.

Colin jerks me back. "Don't come near her."

I hush him. "Is your father responsible for hunting Gypsies like me and taking my father?"

He shakes his head. "No, we only hunt werewolves. He wouldn't..." Kyle bites his lip.

"You're not sure, are you?" I ask.

Howls erupt in the distance.

Colin looks in their direction. "We need to set our differences aside and get Elysia and her cousins out of town now."

"This isn't over." Kyle lowers his gun and takes out his phone.

"Wait, Kyle. Don't call your father, yet. Nadya thinks she found my dad. Please let me see where he is. Maybe you can get some answers, too." The rain slows.

The howling intensifies. Colin pushes me to his truck. "If we don't get out of here soon, a lot more people will die."

***

"This is awkward." Kyle looks out the passenger window. His Jeep wouldn't start, so we piled into Colin's truck after they had pushed the Jeep to the side of the road.

"Thank you both for setting aside your hate." I clasp my hands in my lap. "I know this isn't over, but right now all I want to do is find my dad."

"You need to get out of town." Colin grips the steering wheel tighter. "This isn't a joke, Elysia. They're coming and they will kill you."

"I won't let that happen." Kyle grits his teeth.

Colin snorts. "You don't know what you're up against."

"I can take care of myself," I say. "I'm not going anywhere until I find him." I want to grab hold of

Colin's hand, but don't want to make Kyle uncomfortable.

"It's not the time to be stubborn," Colin says.

He pulls into the campground and slows. Deena's lying on the ground in front of the office.

"Oh my God! Let me out." I push Kyle out of the passenger door. Deena's covered in dirt. I lift her head and place it on my lap.

"Is she okay?" Kyle asks. "Feel for a pulse."

"She's breathing." I shake her lightly. "Deena?" There's a huge red mark on the left side of her face. "Someone hit her with something."

"That's not all they did." Colin stares at the cabin. The door sways in the wind. "I don't have a good feeling about this."

"Alice." Deena's voice startles me and I look down. She blinks several times as if she's trying to focus. "I'm...so—so—rry" she stammers. "I couldn't stop them." Kyle helps her to her feet. She wobbles.

"Get her a chair." I point to the wooden chair near the office entrance.

"I'm fine...or maybe not." Deena reaches up and touches the ugly mark on the side of her head. She eases into the chair.

Once Deena seems like she's okay, I take off toward the cabin. "Fonso! Nadya!"

"Wait!" Colin calls after me, but I keep running.

"Fonso." The cabin's been ransacked. Fonso and

Nadya's clothes are thrown around the room. "Nadya!" No answer. They're gone.

"Elysia!" Colin runs in. "What if there was someone waiting in here for you?"

"They're not here." I run down the hall. The drawers are out of the chest, and my clothes have been tossed all over. "What were they looking for?"

"Fonso's car is still here." Colin points out the window. "Someone took them."

Crackling waves of light dance through the sky.

"Who took them?" Anger boils within me. My brain feels like it's on fire.

Colin embraces me.

Deena appears in the doorway. "It was a woman and a man. They drove a black Mercedes. I didn't get the license plate number. The woman got out of her car and popped me one."

"What did she look like?" Kyle asks from behind her.

"Black hair with short bangs. Wearing leather pants." Deena touches her brow. "Nasty bitch. And, who the hell wears leather pants in this heat?"

"I know her. She's..." I sit on the edge of the couch.

"Vadoma." Kyle says. "Dad is involved. Vadoma is his pet...my ex."

"Your ex-girlfriend? She's the one who kidnapped my father and came after me in New

Orleans." I'm more than shocked by his admission. My head feels woozy and I'm glad I was already sitting or I'd be on the floor. Small cyclones of wind mimic my dizzying head just outside the cabin.

"Why are they going after them?" Colin asks.

"I don't know," Kyle snaps. "He was traveling for a while. I thought he was tracking the wolves."

"And your ex, who is career driven. This is her career?" I ask.

"She hates werewolves more than I do. They killed her entire family." Kyle shakes his head. "I don't understand why she is involved in kidnapping Roma. She's one herself."

"Werewolves?" Deena's eyes widen. She looks back and forth between Colin and Kyle. "I think I may still be knocked out. This is crazier than my nightmares. Then again, I'm pretty sure I saw Fonso throwing rocks through the air without actually picking them up. It's been a hell of a day."

"Where are they?" I glare at Kyle.

"Dad's compound is on the beach. He's got to be there." Kyle steps aside to allow Deena to leave.

"I'm getting a drink." Deena says.

"Let's go." I follow Deena out the door. She walks to her trailer and disappears inside.

"Wait." Colin squeezes my shoulder. "It's too dangerous. We need to get you out of town first, where you'll be safe. I'll go with Kyle to rescue your cousins and dad."

"You'd be committing suicide." Kyle's mouth twitches. "He'd kill you on the spot."

"We are going together." I glare at them both. "I knocked your ex out once before. I can do it again."

"You did?" Kyle smirks. "I would have loved to have seen that."

"It's not safe," Colin insists. "Please."

The look in his pleading eyes would haunt me forever, but I have to go. "It's my family they have. I will get them back." Thunder booms overhead. "I know it's asking more than I should, but I need you there with me." I touch Colin's face.

"Stop petting the dog already." Kyle rolls his eyes.

Colin growls.

"Kyle, I don't know how to say this." I don't even want to say it, but I don't want to give him any more false hope.

"I get it, you're with him." Kyle brows furrow. "Regardless of all the bad things he's done? Roger? My mother?"

I shake my head. "I can't explain—"

"There's nothing to explain." He starts for Colin's truck. "If we're going to do this, we need to move now."

"The packs are coming. I can feel them." Colin grabs my hand and leads me to the truck.

"This isn't going to be pretty," Kyle says.

As we near the truck, three wolves emerge from the surrounding woods. They transform before our eyes.

CHAPTER 23

"COLIN, YOUR FATHER'S arrived," Kayla says, standing stark naked. "He sent us to find you."

"Where's Emilian?" Colin's expression hardens.

"He's safe," Riley says. "We sent him south to the glades cabin. He gave us a hard time about it, too. He made us promise to protect his brother, sister, and her." He nods in my direction.

"How he expects us to do that is beyond me." Brayden walks closer. He seems more confident and open. He stands straight while the others maneuver themselves to block their private areas. "We are merely puppets on a string."

"He wants you to come now," Kayla says. "He says we are at war. A Rom girl killed your Uncle Silas. He's angry you're not already by his side. He's been calling you all night. Why haven't you come?"

The three of them wait to hear his explanation.

"Did you hear his call?" Brayden asks.

"I did." Colin grabs my hand. "I'm not fighting his war anymore."

"What the—" Kayla stares at our united fingers. "I don't understand. Are you and her..."

Their faces turn blank.

"I can't explain it, but being around Elysia breaks the bond." Colin's eyes meet mine. He beams.

"Impossible," Riley says.

"I'm not going back. I'm not extorting. I'm not killing. I'm not going to do his bidding anymore." Colin moves a stray hair behind my ear. "It's over."

"What about us?" Brayden complains. "We've been together for years, we're your family. Her," he jabs a finger in my direction, "This girl is your kryptonite. She's going to get you killed by your own kind."

"We are family. We are also pawns. I know you don't like what my father forces us to do anymore than I do. So why don't you come with us and help find her family," Colin pleads. "We need to get them out of town before more die. Then, if you want, you can go back and tell him I'm gone." His fingers tighten, squeezing my hand. "You're all Emilian's friends and you promised him."

"We did," Kayla says.

Colin lets go of my hand. He reaches behind the seat of his truck, and returns with a bag of clothes. He tosses the bag toward them and they dress quickly.

"If he calls, we'll have to go." Riley zips his jeans up.

"I know," Colin says. "I appreciate your help. It won't be easy." He looks at Kyle. "We're going up against werewolf killers."

"Is that so?" Brayden laughs.

"I never thought I'd see the day. Werewolves, Roma and, Diner Boy fighting side-by-side." Kayla winks at Kyle. "How'd you get involved, anyway?"

"Colin killed my mother." Kyle gives me a sideways glance. "And he stole my girl."

"Tough breaks, kid." Brayden smacks him on the back.

Kayla bores in to me. "For the record, I'm doing this for Emilian. Not for you."

"Yeah, I got it." I roll my eyes.

"What's the plan?" Riley asks. "Storm the castle, rescue the Gypsies? That sort of thing?"

"I don't know of any other plan," Colin says. "Let's go." He hoists me up into the truck.

The others pile into the back. I can't help but think about what kind of father Colin has. I can't say I'm anxious to meet him. He'd likely want to kill me on sight. Kyle's father isn't a saint either, especially having kidnapped my family. Dad never told me anything of my family or who was hunting us, although I have an inkling he knew more than he said. "It seems we are all trapped in our parent's battles."

CHAPTER 24

A
S WE PULL out of the campground, Colin
brakes fast to avoid hitting two
figures...Aunt Simza and Aunt Mirela. Their
colorful, flowing skirts dance in the breeze; their
jewelry gone.

"This keeps getting better and better." Brayden
throws his arms up. "Let's pick up every Rom from
here to Timbuktu. I'm sure it wouldn't attract any of
the pack whatsoever."

"We don't have time for this." Colin stares at me.

"We can help," Aunt Simza says. "Your mother
sent us."

Aunt Mirela glances at Aunt Simza.

"Get in." Colin waves them in.

Kyle climbs in the back to make room for my
aunts in the front.

"Add in a few more people and we can officially
say we've been in a clown car." Brayden lets Kayla

sit on his lap.

"Put the address into my GPS." Colin hands Kyle his phone.

"Now, you want to help?" I say. "You couldn't have given me a hand when I first arrived?" I glare at Aunt Mirela. "You're the reason my father was taken. All these years, you've been helping them find us."

"I didn't know about you. I swear it." Aunt Mirela grabs Aunt Simza's hand. "It was a mistake. One I deeply regret."

"Why did you do it? Why go after my father?"

"She did it to keep Bo away from us." Aunt Simza throws her hand up. "I'm here, aren't I?" she says into the air. She sounds like she's been bewitched.

"Is anyone else following this?" Brayden asks.

"Lyuba says hello and that you're very beautiful and blah blah blah." Aunt Simza sticks her tongue out. "Are you happy now?"

"I'm lost," Riley says.

Colin squeezes my hand.

Aunt Mirela closes her eyes. "A man came to me several years ago. He said he would tell Bo, our father, your grandfather, where we were unless I agreed to tell him where Harman was. Needless to say, it made me nervous. I didn't know where he was and I didn't care to know after your mother died. He ran off, probably as scared of Bo as we were.

Anyway, Nadya has a gift. I used it to keep us safe."

"And to get money out of it." Aunt Simza crosses her arms.

"Simza found out a few months ago," Aunt Mirela says. "She can hold a grudge."

"Fine!" Aunt Simza yells. "Lyuba says we are wasting time. She says they have Fonso, Nadya, and Harman in one room. She can lead us there, but we will need a distraction."

"This is better than a damn soap opera," Riley says. "The Days of a Rom's Life."

"If my mother is helping you, why didn't you come to me sooner?" I ask. "You could have said something when I arrived."

"Simza has her own secrets," Aunt Mirela says. "She never told me about your mother appearing to her, so we are even as far as that's concerned."

"When Lyuba first appeared to me, it was the day you were born. That's when I knew she had died. We knew nothing about you. I didn't see her again until a couple of weeks ago." Aunt Simza faces me. "At the beginning, she didn't say anything. It's hard for spirits to cross planes. It took some time for her to become verbal. Once she did, I couldn't get her to shut up. That's why I sent the note and called you in New Orleans."

"That was you."

"When I found out your father had kept you away

all these years, and that Mirela was being paid to disclose his whereabouts. I became livid and cross. I blocked your mother out," Aunt Simza says.

"You blocked everyone out," Aunt Mirela gripes.

"Lyuba is as stubborn dead as she was alive. Ever since your arrival, she's been pestering me. She even showed up in my damned shower." Aunt Simza rolls her eyes.

"But, you ignored her, and me?" I ask.

"She wasn't the only visitor I've been getting. I've had spirits from all over the world talk with me, in languages I couldn't understand. It was overwhelming. I knew you were trouble right off the bat." Aunt Simza leans back. "I wanted to leave. It's the first time I've hated my gift."

"You didn't tell me that," Aunt Mirela says. "Why did that happen?"

"Some warning about a storm," Aunt Simza explains. "I couldn't understand it half the time. I ignored them like I did Lyuba."

"How did my mother die?" I ask.

"She says it wasn't your fault." Aunt Simza pauses. "There was an earthquake."

I shudder.

"Something fell on her. A beam in the bedroom, I think." Aunt Simza blinks, wiping her eyes. "She says it wasn't your fault."

It was my fault. Large raindrops hit the

windshield.

"She's gone," Aunt Simza says. "She vanished."

"Now?" Colin asks. "Don't we need a guide here? We're almost there."

"There's only two rooms they can be in and it's on the south side," Kyle says.

"She's back," Aunt Simza says.

"Weirdest family ever. And, here I thought shifting into a furry animal was weird." Brayden says.

"Fonso and Nadya are still in the room, surrounded by books," Aunt Simza says.

"The library," Kyle says. "We have to go in the south entrance, on the ocean side. You'll need to go down several blocks and turn around. We have to be able to get away and it's a dead end."

"Where's my father?" I ask.

Aunt Simza shakes her head. "She didn't see him. They must have taken him somewhere else."

Colin turns the truck around at the dead end. Kyle points to a spot on the side of the road and Colin parks.

I'm nauseous. I glance out the window to see the waves churning and slashing against the shore.

Colin rubs my thigh. "We'll find him," he whispers.

Kyle points to a large colonial structure. "That's the house."

"That's a fucking mansion." Kayla's eyes widen. "On the friggin beach, too."

"I'm guessing we are the distraction?" Brayden asks.

"I'll go in the front and divert them." Kyle scoots up on the edge of the seat, closer to us. "Keep them busy for a while. The wolves can go to the north side. Knock over garbage cans, but wait ten minutes. Throw rocks in the windows and run. There's a stone garden near the service entrance. Seriously, get out as quickly as you can. They will chase you...with guns."

Riley looks at his watch. "Okay."

"Colin stays with me," I say. He's the only thing keeping my emotions from going all over the place and causing chaos.

Kyle points to the beach access sign. "When you have them, go to the beach and head south. It'll bring you back to a path that will lead you here. If I don't come back, leave. I'll be fine and I can distract them so you'll get away."

"Thank you, Kyle." He avoids eye contact. It hurts, but it's to be expected.

"You're welcome. I'm sorry this happened. I didn't know, and still don't know why he would take your father. It doesn't make sense." Kyle shakes his head. "Anyway," he looks at each person in the group, "are we clear on what everyone needs to do?"

"Your mother will guide us to the room," Aunt

Simza says.

"Right." Kyle's forehead creases. His hand brushes my shoulder. "Then, you get her out of town."

Kyle and Colin exchange stares for a moment too long.

"I'll get her out of town," Colin says.

We all climb out of the truck.

"Ten minutes," Kyle repeats and walks toward the house.

"Kyle." Colin jogs to him. They exchange words I can't hear. Colin clenches his fists. He watches the ground. Then, returns to my side.

"What was that about?" I ask.

"He's never going to forgive me." I see the turmoil in his face, and it pains me knowing he'd regret what he had done for the rest of his life. He pushes past the moment and waves the others over. "Cross the street and cut back on the opposite side of the house. Ten minutes."

"Why are we doing this again?" Kayla asks. "We don't owe them anything. They've been nothing but trouble to us and if your father finds out, we're dead."

"Have you felt his pull since we've been with them?" Riley asks.

"No," Brayden replies.

"No," Kayla says.

"Me neither," Riley says. "Maybe whatever is

working on Colin is working on us when we're around her." Colin and the others stare at me. "Since the pack arrived, I've heard everything in their minds. But now, I can't hear anything."

"What are you saying?" Colin asks.

"Maybe that's her gift. She's detaching us somehow." Riley pulls his fingers apart. "I don't know how to phrase it."

"She's our way out. Other than being exiled, she's like a golden ticket to freedom," Brayden says.

"Sorry, but she's not going to be your shield." Aunt Mirela grabs my shoulders.

"It's time," Aunt Simza says breaking into their conversation. "We need to go."

They don't waste any time. Riley, Brayden, and Kayla run across the street. Kayla glances back at me. Her eyes light up. For once, it's not hate I see in them, it's hope.

Colin grabs my hand and leads me up the sidewalk.

We push through a hedge, following Aunt Simza. We duck down on a stone path. A small bush covers us. Glass doors line the front part of the house. It's broken up in three sections...a north wing, a central section, and a south wing.

Kyle must have gone in.

My heart races.

"Move." Aunt Simza rises, walking down the

path that leads to the south end of the house.

Gray clouds loom overhead. Colin's touch...his nearness soothes me, somehow. They may think I'm a buffer to their werewolf bond, but in reality it's Colin who's saving them all by helping me control my erratic gift.

We near a side door surrounded by tall hedges. Aunt Simza tugs at it. "It's locked," she whispers to the hedge next to her. To anyone else, that would seem strange.

Clashing sounds begin on the north side. Aunt Simza picks up a rock and knocks out a small glass square window on the door. She cuts her hand as she unlocks it from the inside.

Hooting, hollering, and howling echo on the wind. Riley, Brayden, and Kayla are doing their parts, but I hope they start running like Kyle told them to.

Colin stops Aunt Simza from entering first, and he takes the lead.

He walks down a hall to where Aunt Simza directs him and points to a closed door. He eases it open. Glass doors line the east side, overlooking a kidney-shaped pool with the ocean beyond. Nadya and Fonso are in the center of the room, bound in chairs, their backs to each other. Fonso's out cold. Kyle jumps up, pulling his gun. Recognition lines his face and he holsters it.

"Hurry, we don't have much time." Kyle kneels by Nadya, undoing ropes.

"Ma." Nadya's eyes widen. Tears fall down her cheeks. Aunt Mirela hugs her.

Colin unties Fonso's ropes. His head lulls to the side and he's unresponsive to us.

"Fonso?" I lean down next to him.

"They keep him knocked out," Nadya's voice cracks.

"Shh." Aunt Mirela whispers and helps Kyle.

"Ma, he's got powers," Nadya says "Big powers. They're scared of him."

"Not now Nadya," Aunt Simza peeks down the hallway.

"How will we get him out?" I ask Colin.

"We carry him." Kyle finishes untying Nadya.

Nadya jumps up, embracing Aunt Mirela.

"We need to go." Kyle helps Colin lift Fonso up. "This way." Kyle nods toward the glass doors. "The beach."

I rush to the door to open it for them. Aunt Mirela, Nadya, and Aunt Simza follow them out. I take the rear. We walk around the south end of the pool, pass a cabana, and head toward the beach.

Thunder rolls through the clouds.

Nadya whimpers.

"Wait." Aunt Simza's face turns white. "Something's wrong." She shakes her head. "I can't make it out. Lyuba says we're in trouble. We need to run."

A back door on the other side of the pool crashes open. The raven-haired bitch walks out, pointing a gun at us. She fires.

The shot hits the cabana's wooden boards.

Nadya screams.

We run.

Another shot rings out, but doesn't hit anywhere near us.

I shake with fear. A howling wind swooshes in.

I tumble forward, plunging into Aunt Simza, who has stopped on the beach.

They've all stopped. Colin and Kyle sit Fonso down. Aunt Mirela blankets a shivering Nadya in her arms. All of them are looking in the same direction.

I turn to see what stopped them. On the beach, 50 feet away, a man holds a gun to my kneeling father's head.

CHAPTER 25

MY DAD'S EYES water when he sees me. His hands and feet are tied. He mouths one word to me. "No."

"What do you think you're doing?" Kyle yells.

"What am I doing?" Kyle's dad asks. "You're the traitor. Why are you helping them?" He waves the gun at us. He's an older version of Kyle with less definition in his torso.

"I knew it." The raven-haired bitch Vadoma slinks around us, her gun raised. She shoves Kyle forward as she passes. "He's not cut out to protect the innocent. He's weak."

I glare at her. "You're pathetic without your gun, if I remember correctly."

Colin grabs my arm.

"That's the girl he wanted, right?" Kyle's dad motions to Vadoma. "Take her and get out of here."

A tall, brawny gray-haired man walks down the

shore. "What's going on? What are you doing?"

Aunt Mirela gasps.

"Bo, you dirty ass!" Aunt Simza exclaims. "Figures you're behind this. Why didn't you tell me?" Simza asks the wind. "You didn't think we needed to know this!"

"We found them." Kyle's dad points at me. "There's the girl."

"You kidnapped them?" Bo asks.

"Like you care how they do things." Aunt Mirela spits.

"By any means necessary," Vadoma says. "That's what you said." She steps toward me. "Why you want her, I have no idea, Grandfather."

Aunt Mirela and Aunt Simza stare at each other.

"You've used me all these years," Aunt Mirela says. "And you've used this poor girl, too, haven't you? What did he make you do for him?"

"You said she died." Aunt Simza tears up.

Aunt Simza and Aunt Mirela position themselves in front of me, blocking me. Aunt Mirela pushes Nadya behind her to stand next to me. Nadya grips my hand.

"You're not going to use our children like you used us," Aunt Mirela says.

Riley, Brayden, and Kayla run up the south side of the beach. They slow when Vadoma points the gun in their direction.

"Who the fuck are they?" Vadoma steps back.

Kayla growls at her.

"They're fucking werewolves." Vadoma's eyebrows rise as she looks at Kyle. "You brought fucking werewolves with you?"

"It's not what you think, Mirela." Bo holds his hand up. "Use your head for once and figure it out. When she was born, the earthquake killed Lyuba."

Vadoma trembles. Her face reddens.

Kyle watches her, then turns his attention to his father.

Kyle's father squints, looking at Colin. Recognition dawns on his face. "It's him."

Kyle's father pushes Dad over in the sand. He raises his gun, stepping toward us. He points it at Colin and fires.

"No!" I yell.

Brayden pushes Colin, but he's not quick enough. The bullet pierces his side. He falls.

Kyle tackles his father, causing the gun to fire in the air.

Heat rises inside me. Nadya snaps her hand away, shaking it. Dark skies move in over the water. Howls erupt all around us. At least 50 wolves move in from all directions.

"No, no." Colin holds his side, watching the red eyes encircle us. He seizes Brayden. "Get them out of here. Save Elysia."

Brayden nods.

"Colin?" I kneel. He takes my arm, gazing at me, then closes his eyes and falls limp.

"No!" Fury boils within me.

The wolves growl, moving closer. One howls.

Brayden flinches. "He's asking us to shift and kill you."

Kayla growls. Her clothes rip off as she transforms in front of us. She takes a fighting stance, but instead of attacking me, she faces the incoming wolves.

"She's resisting," Riley says.

"It's working. They don't know what to think." Brayden rips his shirt off, joining Kayla. Riley follows suit.

The other wolves step back. One whimpers.

"Elysia!" Father calls to me. He's the furthest away, struggling with his restraints. A wolf nears him.

A lawn chair flies through the air, knocking the wolf away.

Fonso is weary, but on his feet. He's leaning on Aunt Simza; his arm swings in the air and hurls another chair at a gray wolf. Aunt Simza rushes to untie my dad's legs. He stands. They back up to us, facing the wolves.

"Elysia, calm down." Dad's words echo on the wind.

"Calm down?" I ask. "No."

Aunt Simza grabs my arm, but quickly pulls away, the heat writhing through my veins is too much for her.

Kyle's father throws Kyle over his shoulder, reaching for his gun.

The winds pick up, blowing sand in the air. The ocean water recedes further from the shoreline. Thunder booms.

Fonso continues flinging any lose object he finds through the air, keeping the wolves at bay. Sweat drips down his forehead.

Kyle's father lifts the gun. "I will die today, but I'll go out killing as many of them as possible." He aims at Riley.

Time slows for me. I feel the wind racing through the trees...the dark clouds loom over us, the vibration of the thunder battling above. A hundred waterspouts form in the ocean, dancing on the waves. I take it all in, becoming one with the storm. I allow it to breathe through me. My feet leave the sand, as the wind lifts me up.

Everyone freezes, gawking at me.

A surge of energy enters me from above, followed by the brightest light. I narrow my sight on Kyle's father and lightning bolts from my hands and into his chest.

Vadoma's next. I set my sight and her. She

trembles.

"Elysia! Don't! She's your sister!" Dad blocks her. I couldn't have heard him right. A fogginess numbs me as I try to process his words, but the howling of wind scrambles their meaning.

Listen to your father. A beautiful glowing woman whispers on the wind. *Save them Elysia.*

The whirling gust feels my emotions and builds a sand wall around my family.

The wolves stop their pursuit of the others. A large black wolf growls. The others follow his lead. They move closer toward me.

"They're going after Elysia!" Fonso yells through the roaring squall.

"Get back!" My father herds my family and friends off the shore.

Fonso struggles against him, but my father pushes him away.

Riley and Brayden change into their human form and move Colin off the sand.

Waterspouts encircle several wolves, pulling them through the air. The angry water swoops in around me on both sides, crashing against the pack. It sucks most of them into the dark depths of the ocean. The few remaining wolves scatter from the shore, away from us.

The wind lowers me onto the sand and the surge releases me. I feel the separation as I part from the elements. A sadness sweeps in, replacing the amity I shared with the forces of nature.

Dad catches me before I hit the sand.

"Why did the wolves go after her?" I hear Nadya ask through my haze.

"Because she alone can break the Roaming Curse," Bo says.

CHAPTER 26

SEVERAL PEOPLE SURROUND me, but their faces are a blur. Colin passes in and out of consciousness. Rain starts and stops periodically. Every time he wakes, he squeezes my hand. I refuse to let it go.

On arrival, the paramedics put Colin on a gurney and I'm forced to let go of his hand as they rush him to the ambulance.

Silence is deafening when riding to the hospital in the hopes of saving a life.

Someone leads me inside to a chair in a waiting area. Big arms cradle me. I sink into his chest. "Dad." My voice cracks.

"I'm here. Shhh." He rocks me.

Rain pounds the building, curving sideways hitting the clear windows. It calls to me... whispering its need to fall.

"I'm sorry." A rough voice breaks the silence. Bo,

my grandfather, sits across from us. "I didn't intend for any of this to happen."

"What exactly did you think would happen?" Aunt Mirela asks. "You kidnapped my children."

"That wasn't supposed to happen." He glances at Vadoma standing at the window. "I just wanted to find Elysia."

"How is she my sister?" My throat aches. I'm parched.

"A few years before you were born, Lyuba was pregnant. It was before she met Harman. She was nineteen." Aunt Simza says and takes my right hand. "Tom, the father, ran off before she gave birth. He wasn't Rom. He worked for Bo, helping with security for the shows he put on featuring your mother."

Vadoma turns away from the windows and studies me.

"I didn't tell her about this," Bo says, watching Vadoma.

Aunt Mirela glares at him. "I'm sure there's a lot of things you neglected to tell her."

"She gave birth to a stillborn girl at home. I was there. The baby came out blue." Aunt Simza cries. "How is it possible she's standing here now?"

Everyone's attention turns to Bo.

He clears his throat. "She was dead. I brought Vadoma out of the room so you could console your sister. I kissed her cheek and she started coughing. I almost brought her back into the room, but I couldn't. Lyuba was too young. The child wasn't full Rom. I thought she'd be better off in the hands of other caring parents."

"That wasn't your decision to make." Aunt Simza clenches her teeth. "That almost destroyed her."

A tear runs down Vadoma's cheek. She catches me staring and faces away from me.

"She saved me," Bo says. "When you all left, she was there. Your cousins raised her, until werewolves killed them. She was away at school. It's been us for the last fifteen years."

"You used her to find us?" Aunt Simza asks.

"No. I found you all years ago. I hired a private detective," Bo says. "I left you at peace and helped you from afar when you needed it."

"Helped us?" Aunt Mirela asks. "You made Nadya try to find Harman every year since she was five."

"That's regrettable." Bo creases his brows. "I was curious to see why he fled. I learned of Lyuba's pregnancy and her death. The earthquake. When I arrived to see for myself, I found her, but no baby. Harman had fled."

Dad repositions himself in the chair. "Lyuba asked me to. She knew Elysia was special. She named her in her last breath...it means *lightning struck*."

A silence falls over the room. I clench my fists, thinking how my mother knew me so well from the moment I was born.

Bo clears his throat. "When I found you guys working in one of those nasty carnivals, the detective said you pretended to talk to the dead, tell past lives and find things. I knew what Mirela and Simza did, but the finding things was new. That's when I hired Brian. He used you to locate Harman, but he was always out of reach, thanks to his gift...until now."

"Brian...Kyle's dad," I say. "Where's Kyle?"

Riley, Brayden, and Kayla sit on the far side of the waiting room. Fonso and Nadya sit on the other side of Aunt Mirela and Aunt Simza. Kyle's nowhere to be seen.

"He stayed behind," Dad says.

"You killed his father," Vadoma says from across the room. "Do you blame him?" She scrutinizes me. "You almost killed me."

"He shot Colin," Kayla says.

"Because he killed Brian's wife," Vadoma replies. "Damn werewolf."

Kayla growls.

"Enough," Aunt Mirela says. "Hasn't there been enough fighting and killing for the day?"

"She's right," Aunt Simza says. "It's time to stop fighting amongst ourselves. There's a bigger threat coming and if we don't unite, it'll be the end of all of us."

"What do you mean?" Dad asks. "What's coming?"

Aunt Simza stares at me. "Lyuba says now that the packs know what you can do, they'll be coming for you...for all of us. They won't stop until you're dead or until you break the curse."

"What curse?" I ask.

"The Roaming Curse. It's the reason we are never able to stay in one place for very long. It's also what the wolves are sworn to protect," Bo says. "You're the only one who can break it, which means you're the one the Hunters will be after."

A storm swells in my chest. The overwhelming feeling to protect the ones I love comes over me. The only way to keep them safe is if I leave...alone. A sadness grips me. I just found them, and I wasn't ready to let them go. But, it's the only way.

A doctor walks down the hall toward us. I stand and stare at his expression, trying to figure out the news he has to share before he reaches us.

He stops a few feet away from me. "He's going to be fine," he says and offers a smile. I want to hug him. Tears of joy fall down my face. Bright, glowing, yellow rays stream into the room as a light rain falls.

EPILOGUE
SIX MONTHS LATER

"**E**VERY TIME THEY go to the mainland for supplies, I get nervous," I say.

Colin wraps his arms around me. "I know. Every time you get nervous, the clouds roll in. They'll be fine. Fonso and Harman will be back in less than an hour."

"It feels surreal, all of us being here together, doesn't it?"

Vadoma spars with Kayla at the water's edge on the south side of the island, the only side with a beach. Riley, Brayden, Emilian, and Nadya fish from the dingy. Nadya's crushing hard on Riley. To say that Aunt Mirela isn't happy about it is an understatment. Aunt Simza's working past her anger at Bo. Bo spends most of his time researching, trying to find some solution for breaking this curse.

Colin laughs. "It's utterly bizarre."

"It's so quiet here." I breathe in the salty air.

The orange-reddish sky breaks through the gray clouds as the sun sets. The water beats against the rocks 30 feet below. A fish jumps.

"Hard to believe there's a war raging." Colin kisses me on the cheek.

"I don't want to leave."

"Me neither."

"We have to go soon." I face him. His dark eyes sparkle in the twilight hour. "We are, after all, cursed to roam."

THE END OF BOOK ONE

***

Read the conclusion of The Roaming Curse series by ordering The Hunters' Fate.

www.mirandahardy.com

***

ACKNOWLEDGEMENTS

Lighting Struck has been an incredible book to write, consisting of countless hours of writing, research, and brainstorming.

I'd like to first thank my family, who has allowed me to spend valuable time outside of my regular responsibilities in order to pursue my passions. I love you all very much.

I'd like to thank my editor, Keith B. Darrell, who has taught me many valuable editing strategies. Your patience is appreciated.

A special thanks to Rebecca Frank, who is the wonderful and amazing cover designer. Not only is her work fantastic, but she is a pleasure to work with.

This story has become stronger with the help of my gracious and fabulous beta readers and critique partners. Thank you for your insight.

Thank you to Amy Wright, who is not only my biggest fan, but also my best friend. I wouldn't be where I am without you by my side in this journey.

Finally, I'd like to thank the readers who honor me by reading *Lighting Struck*. Thank you! Thank you! Thank you!

ABOUT THE AUTHOR

MIRANDA HARDY writes literature to keep the voices in her head appeased. When she's not in her fantasy world, she's canoeing in alligator infested waters, or rescuing homeless animals. She goes to coffee shops to do most of her writing while drinking tea. Unable to reveal too much, she has the most boring superpower ever (hint: you have to be a close relative for it to work). She resides in south Florida with her two wonderful children, and too many animals to mention.

Read more from Miranda Hardy

www.mirandahardy.com